PROPHECY:
BLOOD MOON

MADELYNNE ELLIS

When the Blood Moon rises, the demons' prince will wake from his thousand-year slumber and cast a shadow across the sun. The city will become *youkai* paradise, a vast playground of perversity and vice. However, his rebirth will encompass many stages, during which time we will know him only by his mark."

1. WARD BREAKER

**

Copse. OE – (i) A copse, a shackle or fetter for any part of the body.
Also, to secure a prisoner. (ii) A thicket of trees.
Copse-man – One who fetters the dead. fig
-a guardian of mahogany boxes.

**

"BLAZE."

Her voice cut through his waking dream. Were they still walking? He was so numbed by the cold dark of their surroundings the lines between different realities kept colliding in his head. Each vision grew crisper, more vivid than the last. Soon, they'd overwhelm him and then he wouldn't be able to distinguish between the present and what had yet to come.

How long had they been running? His bare feet ached, and his stomach growled, but a wave of nausea drove away the desire to seek out food. Besides, judging by the iron-tinged taste in his mouth he'd recently snacked on something far bloodier than his typical fare of charcoaled beans.

"Blaze, we can stop if you need to rest." Asha stepped in front of him, her face wan, and placed a hand flat upon his naked chest. The action sent a shot of energy through him that raised every hair on his body and instantly sent him tottering back, away from her. She'd helped him escape, but she was still one of them, one of the Talon—the hunters convinced of his demon heritage, and hence intent upon his slaughter. He still wasn't sure he could trust her, even if his body vibrated with need over the thought of her.

Blaze wasn't sure if he could trust anyone anymore, least of all himself.

Who was he?

What was he?

He'd been so certain that he needed to know, but finding Kell's Prophecy—a so called missing chapter from the Apostle's Dialogue that church fools so loved to preach—had changed everything. Now, he wished he could go back, unravel time, forget about discovering his history, and continue to be who he'd always been; a boy from the Birdcage slums, who lived hand to mouth, lined his eyes with kohl and waxed his hair into impressive spikes.

He blinked, trying to rid himself of the kaleidoscope of coloured lights flitting around his head, and then peeped at his inscrutable saviour. She was willowy and cold, yet lovely, exceptionally lovely, especially the bright green of her eyes. In other circumstances, he'd have hit upon her and probably lost his head for the effort. The few stolen tastes of her he'd already had stirred his blood in a way that wasn't natural. She turned him into the beast he feared to become. He looked at her and his heart raced and rational thoughts escaped him. He wanted only to slide into her; possess, taste, devour her, or at least that was how he'd felt until she'd magicked him into obedience.

She'd almost killed the cravings...almost...

Blaze dragged a hand across the design inked across his stomach, faintly sickened by the knowledge that even though she'd freed him from the enscorcelled cage in the cathedral, he was still bound. The new tattoo was holding him in check and preventing whatever metamorphosis had been about to happen.

If only he knew why she'd aided him.

Not out of pity, that was for certain.

The Talon weren't known for their pity. He could only assume she wanted something from him that was worth risking her master's wrath.

"Where are we?" he asked.

"I reckon we've come a mile or two at the most." Despite the stress of their situation, Asha's voice remained calm.

"We're not out of danger yet."

They had to keep moving if he wanted to survive. His survival instinct ran deep.

"Then we're still inside the city?"

Asha inclined her head a fraction, so sections of her long black hair spilled over her shoulders and shrouded the porcelain-white perfection of her face. He didn't think he'd ever get tired of looking at her. She reminded him of a china doll, except there was nothing fragile about her. Beneath the scalloped lace and funereal gown lay a ruthless, battle-hardened warrior. Dolls, or Talon's Dolls, were what the population called the elite demon hunters, because they looked like marionettes. Not that they were ever called that to their faces. Few folks stopped for a chat with the Talon. Doing so usually led to an early grave.

"There's daylight ahead. We'll find out soon enough where we are."

Daylight! Had one day bled into another? Twenty-four hours since he'd found that pamphlet and unwittingly drawn the attention of both the youkai and the Talon.

Disoriented, he stumbled over a rock.

Asha caught hold of his elbow and guided him along the path. "Blaze, I know you're tired, but stay with me." The soles of his feet were torn and bruised, but her touch somehow brought relief. Strength seemed to permeate his limbs when she held him, and warmth crept through his veins, spurring him so that they pushed on a little further.

He thirsted for a glimpse of the sun, and yet, here in the darkness they were safe. Beyond the tunnel mouth, he couldn't predict.

There were bars across the exit, with a gate fastened by a rope of chain and a hefty padlock. Asha took a pin from her hair, but the lock crumbled into dust at the first touch.

"That makes it easier." Her words were jocular, but no expression registered on her face.

Blaze gave her a nervous smile.

He let the suns golden rays stripe his feet first, and only once they'd thawed and a little heat ran through his veins did he venture further into the light.

"It's clear," Asha called back to him.

Yellow-grey buildings surrounded the tunnel mouth. They stood in a small cobblestone courtyard pitted with weeds. The remains of a mill-wheel stood propped against one wall, while ahead lay the canal. On the other side of the water, derelict warehouses were squashed together like slumbering behemoths.

"How can we be here?" Blaze shook his head in dismay. "This is the copse road." They were in smelling distance of the crossroads and its swinging iron gibbets. The piercing clank of their thick chains ran though the still air like a doomsday alarm clock, reminding him of the nightmare dead he saw in his dreams, spewing from the open cages.

The dreams had been what'd driven him to seek out that blasted book. Dreams and... He wrinkled his nose, disgusted that he'd placed such importance on knowing who had sired him, given they'd abandoned him at birth.

As if it mattered.

As if any of it mattered...

What had he even learned? Nothing he actually wanted to know. It wasn't as if he welcomed the thought of being a demon, or having demon blood, or whatever the hell it was everyone suspected.

"We've circled round. This tunnel must have carried things between the canal and the station at some point."

Some point so long ago no one could remember it. The only trains that ran these days operated out of the Heights, and lord knows where they went, some idyllic paradise for all he knew. He'd never set foot outside the city. Maybe that's where he should be headed, out into the wasteland, as far as he could go, away from those who wished him harm.

"I thought we'd at least be outside the city walls." He sagged onto his bottom on the quayside and dangled his feet into the dingy water. Asha squatted on one knee beside him, so that her dark skirts fanned over the cobbles. She pressed a gloved hand to his shoulder.

"Perhaps we're not meant to leave. There's little out there and dressed as you are, I'm not sure how long you'd survive. You need more than a pair of leather trousers to brave the wasteland, Blaze."

He shivered, acutely aware of how vulnerable his near nakedness left him. They needed to make clothes—boots, especially—a priority.

"Best we lay low for a while, and keep you out of sight." Asha's gaze drifted towards his chest, where the smooth, swirling lines of a raised brand marred the pale skin. He didn't know what it was meant to be, but it always reminded him of fire.

Blaze self-consciously covered the mark with his palm. It made his skin itch just to have someone look at it. Everything had started with its appearance, after he'd read that damned book—the visions, the strange cravings, his wings.

Perhaps he had only dreamt the last part, and soaring above the city plaza.

Maybe he was dreaming even now. The world around him and the people in it all seemed unhinged enough to be figments of his imagination. Maybe he was still inside that Talon cage, or perhaps he'd never got away with the stolen book in the first place and someone had brayed him across the head and he'd wake up soon, in a cell, up on a charge of petty theft.

The latter was wishful thinking and he knew it.

Asha's shadow moved across the surface of the water as she rose. Blaze noticed several strands of hair had worked free of the elaborate braids that formed a crown around the top of the glossy mane.

Fuck! He didn't want to run anymore, only to sleep off the hurts to his limbs and his heart.

Dare he trust her—this beautiful, poised, and lovely killer?

"Blaze—," She bent over him again. "—best we don't linger. We're exposed here."

They were hemmed in by buildings on three sides and by the canal on the fourth, save for a shallow ledge that led between the water and the edge of one of the buildings. However, Asha's gaze swept skyward, her concern clearly over the winged youkai.

To think, less than twenty-four hours ago, he'd thought the demons little more than a myth designed to keep children away from the crossroads. Hardly anyone had seen one of the youkai, and most of the ones who had, were written off as delusional. The only reason they weren't entirely dismissed, was because of the Talon. Them you took seriously. People stayed clear of them. Folks were more scared of the hunters than they were of the demons. If the Talon so much as suspected you were a demon, you were butchered meat. At least that's how it was told. For some reason they seemed to have broken their own rules with him.

Hence he lived, despite suspicions.

Asha had saved him, not killed him.

There had to be a reason for that.

The words of the ancient prophecy echoed in his head.

When the Blood Moon rises, the demons' prince will wake from his thousand-year slumber and cast a shadow across the sun.

Nope, he still didn't see why anyone would imagine it had anything to do with him.

The city will become a youkai paradise, a vast playground of perversity and vice. However, his rebirth will encompass many stages, during which time we will know him only by his mark.

Fair enough, that bit was the killer. He wished he had something with which to conceal the strange sigil.

"Back to the tunnel?" he asked hopefully, for now darkness would suffice.

The tiniest suggestion of a smile chased across Asha's black-painted lips. "Hiding in the dark won't help. We need answers, Blaze. Answers about what's happening to you." She gave a quick shake of her head. "We need to know who and what you are. What role you're destined to play in all this. Properly armed and forewarned we can derail whatever plans the demon-filth have for you. I'm not ready to accept their rule, are you?"

Interesting question, given that everyone seemed to think he was destined to rule. He couldn't see it himself, not unless they routinely put the most feeble of their kind on the throne. Demons were supposed to be able to fly and shift form at will. He could barely put one foot before the other. And his head... He didn't know where his head was; only that his memory was full of holes.

"Where then?" he asked, hoping she knew of some secret hidey-hole with a feather bed.

"The Birdcage."

"Home?"

Interest piqued, Blaze scrambled to his feet. To his knowledge neither the Talon nor the demons had any presence in the Birdcage, presumably because neither thought the slums worthy of their attention. However, that didn't mean it was safe. Surely there'd be a watch upon his house? "Why?"

"Because you need clothes, pretty as the current view is, and the Eyrie was the main watch post during the last cycle of demon rule. There may be information there we can use. The various archives are out of the question for us right now. They all pay dues to the Talon and know better than to harbour fugitives."

"The Eyrie." Blaze stared at her with his mouth agape, still focused on the start of her explanation. "Isn't climbing to the highest point in the city going to mark us out?"

"There's no reason for anyone to look for you there. You don't have any connection to it."

Well, besides the fact the looming pinnacle stood a mere three streets away from his house, and he'd sometimes hung around there when he had nothing better to do.

He'd rarely had anything better to do.

"Asha, there's no way in. It's a locked box." He'd known plenty of people who'd lusted after its secrets, and seen plenty of fools dissolve into cinders trying to unravel them." He folded his arms across his chest, concealing the raised brand. "Unless, of course, the Talon have keys?"

"I'm no longer part of them, Blaze. I closed that career path the moment I freed you."

He wasn't so sure of that, not considering how she still wore her fanciful outfit like a badge of honour.

"No keys, either." She turned her gloved hands upwards. "But I'm sure we can find a way in. Just tell me what you know."

"What I know, is that anyone who tries to enter it ends up dead."

"Yes, but how?"

Trust a woman to want all the gory details. "Well, in addition to a two-foot thick growth of bindweed covering the place, it's warded. You know the sort—pop, fizzle, croak, dead rat sort of ward."

She pursed her lips, her expression thoughtful. Then he saw it, a brightening of her eyes. For a moment they were luminous; the green so vivid as to be unnatural. "Then it's simple. What we need is a Ward Breaker."

Blaze gave a dismissive snort. "That's what most of the idiots who hurled themselves at the doors claimed to be."

"Yes, but how many of them were actually conversant in the ancient tongues?"

He shrugged. "Most of them could barely manage the common-tongue."

"Quite. What I meant was a real Ward Breaker."

"Yeah," he drawled growing tired again, and wishing a seat would just materialize. "And where are we supposed to find one of those." Ward

Breakers—genuine ward breakers as opposed to petty thieves—were almost as mythical as the youkai. "Unless you have one tucked inside your bodice?"

Asha lifted one of her delicate eyebrows so it formed a haughty arch.

"Not inside my bodice, no. But there is one close by. This way."

She turned, making her dark skirts swirl, and strode off uphill towards the crossroads. Blaze hesitated, and then padded along behind her trying to keep to the shadows. Even in this part of the city, it seemed madness to walk in the open so brazenly.

Asha headed straight for the lich-gate, the carved and scrolled ironwork boundary that separated the Death Ward from the rest of the Old City.

"Asha, wait. I'm not going in there." No one in their right mind went in there. The Death Ward was for the dead. Living things had a habit of dying if they crossed the boundary.

"Blaze, you only get to pass through this gate once. Flat on your back inside a mahogany box. We're merely paying a house call."

She hammered on the monstrous gate, and somewhere high above a lone bell pealed.

Blaze shifted uncomfortably. The doleful, echoic toll made his skin crawl. His gaze moved to the archive building on his left. It all looked so perfectly normal in the daylight, but the dead ruled this place come nightfall. "I don't like it here. We're too exposed."

"A moment longer. It'll be worth it." She clasped his hand, but Blaze shook off the hold.

Hell, just because he hadn't killed a zillion demons, like her, didn't mean he hadn't seen a heck of a lot of violence. He didn't need cosseting just because this place gave him the creeps.

"What do you want, Asha Lemarche?" The unfamiliar voice came from behind them.

Alarmed, Blaze swivelled on the spot, to find a dark robed figure a mere step away. All distinguishing characteristics were hidden by the vast depths of his cowl and his overlarge sleeves, into which his arms were folded. As he watched, ghostly figures chased across the weft of the robe and peeped out at him.

"Fuck!" He back-stepped to stand level with Asha.

"Whatever is this that you've brought me?" The man's hollow voice seemed to reverberate with the same dull tone as the bell Asha had rung.

"Nothing—other than greetings, Vervain. We have need of your service."

"Do you?" His attention turned briefly to Asha. "What manner of service? Not more poor unfortunates you've mistakenly executed thinking them youkai." His penetrating gaze returned to Blaze.

"We need to get into the Eyrie."

"Of course you do." He drew his hood back, revealing a clean-shaven head, olive skin and a long craggy face.

Blaze took another wary step backwards. The man's eyes were like slivers of jet—hard, piercing, and unnatural.

"Talon's mastery of the old tongues far surpasses mine. Have your master open the Eyrie for you."

Vervain made to turn away.

"I cannot."

"Cannot?" Vervain parroted, stilling, though the figures within his robe still moved.

"He fell some hours ago. A spear pierced his chest."

It'd had been their only means of escaping his clutches. There were still traces of blood on Blaze's hands.

Vervain laughed at her. "Do you mean to fool me, a warden of the dead, with your tales of Talon's demise? Why don't you tell me the truth instead, Asha? That you are no longer bound to him. That you're running.' His lips pursed. "He's not dead, Asha, regardless of whatever you say you did or saw. I know the names of every man, woman and child who has passed these gates, and Talon is not among them, so I advise you to run far and run fast."

"I saw him crumple," Blaze swore. He grasped Asha's arm, meaning to reassure both her and himself.

"Fall, perhaps," Vervain agreed. "But not die. He has not passed this gate." He inclined his head towards the towering lich-gate, from beyond which could be heard a baleful keening. "There are few, if any, in this world with the skill to undo him completely. He was old when my father was young, and he knows how to weave words so that the universe sits up and listens. An ordinary spear might stop his heart, but you'll have to do more than that to kill him. But you know this already, Asha. Perhaps you just overlooked mentioning it to your new friend."

"Asha?" Blaze beseeched her.

She waved away his question. "Will you help us, Vervain? Say yay or nay."

Vervain steepled his fingers, revealing large slender hands, the fingertips of which were stained with ink. "Let us speak first of whether I can trust your demon lord to honour a bargain."

Him, a demon lord—seriously? He was beginning to think everyone else saw a very different visage to the one he saw when he looked at himself in a mirror. Blaze flicked his tongue against his eye-tooth, half longing, and half afraid he'd find it grown long and pointy.

It remained the same as ever.

Shame, because he was getting tired of people's responses to him. Biting off heads was starting to grow in its appeal.

Asha leapt forward and caught the cuff of Vervain's voluminous sleeve. "He is not one of them."

"You no more believe that than you do Talon dead. We'll deal honestly, Asha, or not at all. He bears the mark of the royal house. If you are not in allegiance with the enemy, then tell me, what is he?"

Hesitantly, she withdrew her fingers from the fabric. She glanced at Blaze, but refused to meet his eyes. "That's what we need to find out. I have him bound. If he's one of them, then he's safe. Both Talon and youkai think him important."

"Then mayhap you should hand him over to one of them. This cycle of human ascendancy is drawing to a close, Asha. It's not the time for foolish games."

"Please, Vervain."

Vervain smoothed the creases from his robe.

Although his gaze remained centred upon Asha, Blaze's senses tickled as though someone were rubbing an emery board against his skin and with each stroke scraped away a minute piece of information. He bristled with annoyance, and rubbed at the irritation.

"Name your price, copse-man." Asha pushed her way between them, breaking the link.

Vervain's smile broadened enough to show his uneven teeth. "Very well. From you, the bone of the long deceased that calls to me from your pocket, and from him—" He stared at the mark on Blaze's chest as if contemplating. "—his nail clippings and a vial of his seed."

Asha turned to him. "Blaze, do you agree?"

The hell he did.

Blaze shoved his hands deep into the pockets of his leather jeans and stalked off in the direction of home. A barter economy was all well and good—hell, it wasn't as if he had any money—but that didn't mean he was going to humiliate himself or trade bits of himself. Not when he barely knew who the hell he was.

"Blaze?" The clip of Asha's metal heeled boots rang against the cobbles behind him. "Come on, it's a fair trade, and not such an unusual one."

"No." His grandma had warned him about giving away pieces of himself. All right, she'd been thinking in terms of kidneys and whatnots, but still... "Nobody is getting anything from me. Not so much as an eyelash."

Her fingers curled into his shoulder and squeezed, bringing his retreat to a halt. "Blaze, please. This is the only way get inside the Eyrie. If there's any information in there... It could make all the difference... And Vervain is the only genuine Ward Breaker I know.

"I don't like it."

"I don't like it either, but if Talon catches us, we'll both of us like it even less. He won't cage you a second time, Blaze. He'll put an end to you." Her lips briefly brushed his cheek.

Irritably, he rubbed at the warm spot left behind, wishing it didn't cause his blood to stir so much

'Please, for my sake as much as your own. I've no desire to be dragged before Talon again either. And he won't kill me." Her eyes glittered. Then she lowered her long eyelashes, masking whatever weakness she presumably feared he'd see. "It'll be a hell of a lot worse."

Blaze rubbed a hand across his tired eyes. He owed her, and his grandmother had always taught him to pay his debts, but he still didn't like it. "Very well."

"He'll do it," she called to Vervain, who nodded and tossed them a small vial. The sun glinted off his bald scalp. "You have forty minutes to collect my payment. I'll meet you there. And Asha, be careful. Your pet isn't as tame as he looks, nor will that scribble you have him bound with hold forever."

Blaze instinctively clasped a hand to his stomach, where the intricate tattoo scarred his flesh and held whatever demon blood he had in check. He didn't pretend to know how it worked, only that it seemed to have brought whatever transformation he'd been going through to a halt. He no longer craved raw meat, and his libido had cranked down a notch or two. Not that they'd really put it to the test yet. Sex had triggered every change so far, which was another reason he wasn't so keen to come, be it into a vial or anything else. Though the prospect of maybe getting intimate with Asha, did momentarily raise his spirits.

"I don't want to be one of them." If nothing else the youkai were an ugly bunch in their true forms. Maybe it was narcissistic of him, but he liked looking good. It really pissed him off when you were in a fight and bleeders went for the face. He liked his nice straight nose and his high cheek bones. "You promised me the binding would stop it." It was the only reason he'd tolerated such a shackle.

Asha clasped his hand and squeezed. "You're not one of them. I kill demons, remember, and you're still alive."

2. BLOOD RAIN

"AW, COME ON, Blaze. It's not as if there's no joy to be had out of what he's asked of you," Asha remarked, as they followed the weed grown tow path towards the Birdcage. In all truth, Vervain had let them off remarkably lightly. He could have demanded much more, and normally did, which perturbed her more than a little. It made her wonder what role he intended to take in this game. Neutral friends were useful, but dangerous, more dangerous than enemies in some respects. She never liked not knowing where she stood with someone. Not that she entirely knew where she stood with Blaze.

He glowered sullenly at her, shoulders hunched, and upped his pace so that he pushed on a short distance ahead.

Maybe once he'd pulled on a clean T-shirt and some boots, and poured a hot drink down his throat he'd find his sense of humour. Assuming he had such a thing. She didn't exactly know a whole lot about him; just his worth and his taste, and that their fates were bound whether he realised it or not yet.

Following him at a distance of five paces, Asha rubbed her thumb in a slow circle over her right palm. Beneath the leather glove, her skin itched where a brand, the twin of the one burned into Blaze's chest, scarred her hand.

That was why she'd released him, because she needed answers too.

Well, that and the draw between them. The binding rune had helped temper it, but there remained a distinctive low level erotic burn that snagged her attention and got under her skin in a way she couldn't ignore.

She'd barely looked at any man besides Talon for years, and she only paid her master attention because it was suicidal to do otherwise. Talon was deliberately provocative and he knew exactly how to press her buttons, but she'd never desired him in the way she did Blaze. She'd simply succumbed to his machinations. What she felt for Blaze, when she'd found him locked in that cage caused her whole body to purr. He didn't even have to touch her. The taste, the smell of him, drew her to him. He packed more punch than an illegal high.

He was the ultimate illegal high, and a bad, bad choice, but then her whole life consisted of one stupid decision after another.

If she possessed any sense, she'd lift her sword now and splatter his blood across the broken cobbles. She'd spent enough years of her life hunting youkai, to know the damage they could do, and she knew all the tricks they played, but even though she fingered the hilt of her sword, she knew she wouldn't do it.

Blaze was her salvation

Her ticket to freedom.

For too long she'd been enslaved to Talon's will. Had spent too many nights naked and tormented in that bastard's bed. He'd warped her, bound her too long in a web of sex and addiction. Talon's greatest thrill was to play mind games with those around him.

A stray feather, blown along on the breeze, caught in the waxed spikes of Blaze's hair. She watched him pulled it out and cast it aside. The soft glow of the sun lent warmth to his pale skin, and turned his ash-blond hair silver-white.

She liked that he was pale, like her. Although in his case it was likely from too much nocturnal living rather than the layers of carefully applied paint.

Her gaze drifted over the length of his back, where perfect depictions of black feathery wings were drawn in detail no tattoo artist could ever achieve, to his leather-encased arse. Blaze had just the right amount of bottom to really dig her nails into and squeeze; nicely toned, but not too much muscle. She liked wiry strength, not the disgusting feel of lying prone beneath a one-man juggernaut. Maybe she'd spent too much time amongst the Talon, but she appreciated agility and grace more than brawn.

"Are you watching my back, or contemplating where to stick a dagger?" Blaze looked over his shoulder at her. He paused and waited for her to catch up. "What does he want it for, Asha? My seed, what will he do with it?"

She shrugged. "Ward Breakers are a bit like Alchemists when it comes to bodily fluids. I find it's best not to ask what they want things for. The answer is rarely pleasant. Better just to be thankful he was willing to help."

Blaze sniffed, "What if he's gone straight to Talon and told him our position?"

"He hasn't."

"How can you be so certain?"

"We're still alive, and besides, there's no love lost between Vervain and Talon. They tolerate one another, but rather more importantly, Talon doesn't have anything Vervain wants. He'll honour the bargain, Blaze, as long as we deliver. You can trust in that."

"I don't trust anything."

She wished she could honestly say she was saddened by that fact, but in truth, it was wise, and it wasn't as if she entirely trusted anybody either. She negotiated on the understanding that everyone had their own agenda.

Asha was pulled from her thoughts a few seconds later by the sound of Blaze's chuckle. "What?" she asked, surprised by his laughter.

A broad grin creased his face, drawing attention to the cute little flaw where in the past someone had taken a nick out of his jaw. Smiling made him look younger.

"Just thinking, all those times when I was starving and considered selling myself to make ends meet, I should have just been tossing it into a bottle and selling it. What do you think I'd get, five hundred florins a pop?"

She grimaced, but that only made him laugh harder.

"Did you ever?" she asked. "You know... the former, not the latter."

"Sell myself, you mean? Did you?"

Well, there was a loaded question. Had she sold herself? Perhaps not in the traditional sense, but somehow she'd found her way into the Talon, and it hadn't been by knocking on the cathedral door and asking very nicely if they'd mind training her to decapitate scum. No, the path had been altogether more torturous and crooked than that.

"You can read a lot into a silence."

"Yes, a whole lot of nonsense normally."

They reached the lock and crossed the canal via a rickety five-inch wide bridge, with a handrail on only one side. As they reached the far bank, another feather stuck in Blaze's hair. Asha reached to remove it, only to freeze mid-stretch as a dark shadow sailed across the surface of the still water below.

"Run!" she yelled. Feather forgotten, she thumped Blaze across the back, urging him forward. "Quick, find some cover."

He hesitated.

"Do it, Blaze." She shoved him again, and found herself some solid ground. "I can handle this."

BLAZE LEAPT OFF the far end of the bridge. He didn't look back but dived for cover amongst a pile of abandoned furniture stacked next to an overflowing bin. The stench of rotten fish assailed his nostrils, almost making him gag. He turned his head away from the refuse and huddled behind an overturned sofa riddled with protruding springs.

A horrid screech tore through the sky. The sound reverberated off the side of the building making his ears ache. Blaze shrank back against the damp upholstery, his palm clasped to the demon mark on his chest.

Through a tear in the sofa base he could see Asha. Safely off the bridge, she stood poised on the quayside, as lovely and coldly perfect as she'd been when he'd awoken last night to find her tending his wounds. Although she'd abandoned her fellow demon-hunters, at this moment her Talon mask remained firmly in place.

She was such an intriguing dichotomy. With her stark alabaster-white skin, long raven tresses and her fanciful outfit of velvet and lace, she looked like the beloved concubine of some business magnate from the Heights—an expensive toy cast aside on the riverbank. While in truth, she was an angel of darkness: a passionate and lethal herald of all that had befallen him. Somehow—he didn't pretend to understand how—their fates had become entwined. Without her, he didn't doubt that he'd already be dead.

"Asha," he whispered, but the encouragement was drowned out by a second unholy screech.

A triple shadow rose before her. It approached in a wedge of flesh, scales and fur.

Asha remained perfectly still. Not even the breeze stirred the fabric of her funereal garb. In the space of a blink, she moved. Blaze caught the flash of reflective steel as the first of the youkai lost an arm. It fell squalling to the ground, an amalgam of flesh and quills. Not quite youkai, not entirely human either. The second, she split across the middle, her sword swinging in a single vicious arc. Blood splashed her face and clothing. It soaked into her skirts, the vibrant red running into the weave and transforming the brocade: a new pattern to mark the passing of another foe.

Blaze winced at each gristly smack. His bare back itched as if the skin were about to split. To alleviate the annoyance he rubbed up against the protruding sofa arm, only to stare in shock a moment later. The calls of the youkai were urging him to transform. The sigil prevented him shifting, but in doing so the crudely inked tattoo began to glow bright green.

Frantically, he tried to hitch his leather trousers over the light, but his fingers locked into arthritic claws.

"No," he sobbed.

Heat pulsed through his body, and he began to shake.

Another caw sounded over the canal, and Blaze screamed as the sigil tattooed upon his stomach countered his body's urge to transform. His skin stretched, but it didn't rip to enable feathery appendages to sprout from his back. The agony of it rendered him powerless. He collapsed onto the dirty cobbles, sucking down desperate breaths through his clenched teeth.

Asha backed towards him. She spun, whisper fast. Calm. Precise. Lethal. Her blade flashed, and left streamers of coppery dust behind in its wake.

The third demon gave a baleful squawk, and stretched his feathers. Tawny wings frantically flapped, each beat sending a tide of litter rustling towards him. The youkai tried to soar, seeking freedom amongst the clouds. Asha held it skewered upon the end of her sword, until it burst. Its final form dispersed into a shower of coppery dust.

Then calmly, she returned to the water's edge and stabbed through the heart of the first demon, who still lay hollering at the loss of its limb.

She still performed as one of Talon's dolls.

Remained at core a perfect demon-slaying marionette.

He wondered how soon she'd realise the truth of him and drive her sword-tip through his heart.

"It's done," she called to Blaze, her voice emotionless.

He didn't answer, just continued to clutch his stomach, while staring dazedly at the sky. Slowly, the pain ebbed away. Blaze wiped the sweat from his face and cautiously pushed himself to his feet.

The remains of the youkai lay in two neat powdery piles on the ground. The essence of the third remained suspended in the air as a cloud of coppery particles. The dust would eventually fall, likely onto cotton sheets. The city's alchemists always knew where to find Blood Rain.

"Are you all right?" she asked.

Blaze brushed a soggy piece of newspaper from his shoulder and nodded. He'd worry over his body's reaction to the calls of the other youkai later. Maybe it was just coincidence the two events had happened together.

Asha gave a crisp nod, then gracefully dipped

onto one knee and scooped up a handful of the demon dust. She let it slowly sift between her gloved fingers before running her tongue over what remained upon the middle digit.

"Should you be doing that?" Blaze asked. There was a reason the stuff was illegal. It was highly addictive. A teaspoon's worth purportedly enough to make a love slave of anyone.

Asha's eyebrows twitched and the tiniest hint of amusement lit up her face. She turned her wrist and offered up her remaining fingers for him to suck clean.

Blaze took a wary step back.

"What are you worried about, Blaze? Do you think I'll be so overcome with lust I'll have to pin you to that sofa and tear the remains of your clothes off? Credit me with some resilience."

Still hesitant, Blaze folded his arms across his chest and hugged his biceps. If he'd had boots on, he'd have stomped the damn demon dust into the cracks between the cobblestones, so it couldn't hurt anyone. The only thing Blood Rain had ever done was turn sensible men into sex-craved lunatics. "Asha," he pleaded. How could a demon hunter be so blasé about tasting the stuff?

And yes, that's exactly what he feared. Wasn't it how this trouble had started in the first place? She'd licked his wounds clean, having saved him from a bunch of demons, and then got high on the taste of him. Maybe she'd only freed him because it was her fault he'd been locked up in the first place.

'Demon blood,' she'd realised on tasting him, and then delivered him straight to her master.

Asha blew the remainder of the dust from her

palm. "They were foot soldiers, not out for us specifically, just looking for an easy meal."

"You can tell all that from one taste?"

She gave a terse smile. "Believe me, Talon made sure I was a connoisseur. The high ups taste different. They smell different, too."

She leaned in close and sniffed him. "None of them smell or taste like you."

3. REBIRTH

**

Perversity is in their blood.
They are born of it.
It's all the youkai know.
--Talon's indoctrination speech
**

N AN ABANDONED railway cart across the city, death permeated the air in the form of a noxious metallic scent. On the floor, Talon opened his eyes. He stood and his dark reflection peered back at him from the windows. His blond hair hung loose from its numerous braids. Blood matted the ends making the golden strands appear red. The tendrils clove to his naked chest, where blood lay dried in flaking ribbons.

Talon raised his hands. His fingertips were stained with soot, a sure sign he'd resorted to the old way of addressing the world. He leaned closer to the glass. Something wasn't right. His eyes were changed, their shape more elongated, the pupils now slit like those of a cat.

He remembered dying!

The torturous pain as the halberd pierced his chest, yet there remained no scar on his skin, or any sign of the implement of his destruction. Had his alchemy saved him, the runes that marked his body, or the magic he'd woven with the fledgling youkai prince's essence?

He stretched and two snowy wings fanned from his back.

Talon leaned into the glass again.

How? Then he sensed it, a change. Alien blood stirred in his veins. The remains of the demon, Venom, who had fallen before him had somehow seeped inside him. "Curious." He raised one brow.

This certainly made things interesting.

The era of human dominance was drawing to a close again, the youkai were rising. Soon their prince would be crowned. Talon glanced down at the phases of the moon inked in silver along the inside of his right arm. The Blood Moon was coming. A red blush already clouded the surface of the full moon symbol.

Yet, nothing was set in stone. There were myriad ways in which to fulfil the prophecy, and youkai blood mixed with years of alchemical research would undoubtedly prove efficacious in the endeavour.

He laughed. No dull little youkai prince was going to usurp control of the city from him. He'd spent centuries building his power base. Few realised how far it extended. Not the politicians in the Heights, or the ordinary folk upon whom they preyed.

The youkai were rising, but if there was going to be a paradise of perversity on Earth, it would be a paradise of his making, not the mediocre offering of some idiot boy.

However, first things first. It was time to rally the troops.

4. BIRDCAGE

**

"That the origins of the Birdcage are entwined with demon myth is largely
unknown to the present inhabitants. Though today, as in the past, it is
considered the greatest receptacle in the City for wicked characters."
-Albert Yarrow, Treatise on Rookeries.

**

BLAZE LEFT ASHA standing guard in the hallway of his grandmother's house in the Birdcage, while he raced up the rickety wooden stairs to his turret room. If he could have left her in the street without drawing unnecessary attention, he would have. He hadn't realised it until he reached the front door, but he didn't want Asha coming in here. His grandmother had harboured an inherent, lifelong distrust of the Talon. Of course the reason for it made perfect sense now. She'd been protecting him and their lineage. At the time he'd simply put it down to their ruthless, pitiless natures, and their propensity for violence.

The air was stale on the upper landing. Blaze passed Grandma's room without looking in. He'd left it as she liked it—homely, and immaculate. Hell, he'd even been going in there once a week since her death just to clean. Meanwhile, the rest of the place was slowly disappearing under a blanket of dust. There'd been other things on his mind. Finding out who he was and where he'd come from seemed more important than running a duster over a few surfaces and sweeping up.

If only the old girl were still here now. She'd have known what to do. That was the one constant about her—he could always rely on her to be practical no matter the trauma.

He remembered sitting in her deck chair on their little terrace out back, swinging his legs as she daubed his scrapes with antiseptic, him having just come home with the knees torn out of his trousers again. How long ago had that been? He surely hadn't been more than ten at the time.

'Three or twenty-three, it don't make a difference,' he could hear her saying. He looked up to see the card she'd given him last birthday still hooked behind the mirror on the landing outside his bedroom door. Mirrors were reserved for hallways, and never hung in rooms. Yet another of his grandma's oddities. She'd tried to explain it to him once, but he hadn't really been paying attention—something about soul traps.

How he wished he could wrap his arms around her now, and see a smile light her curiously soft yet wrinkled features. Come the end, all she'd done was sit holding her knitting with a perpetually cooling cup of tea by the bedside.

He should have made time to talk to her more.

"Hurry it up, Blaze," Asha called from downstairs. "Get some clothes and do what you need to and let's leave. This is not a good place to be. It isn't safe."

He snorted in disgust and approached the

mirror. Rather surprisingly, he didn't look as fucked as he felt. Hours of being semi-naked on the streets hadn't treated him kindly, he was bruised and scraped, but while the kohl around his eyes was smeared, his hair was still appropriately swept back and spiky.

Blaze mustered a grin as he retrieved a tub from a shelf below the mirror and scooped another blob of wax into his hands. He re-coaxed a few of the spikes into perfection before stepping back to take a good look at the mess that was his torso.

Friggin' hellfire! He'd never liked the idea of ink and now he was covered in the stuff. Sure, there was artistic merit in the swirling, tumbling lines that covered his abdomen, but just looking at the inhibiting sigil made him want to retch.

Then there was the demon mark just above his breastbone. No one could consider that pretty. It was mottled, strawberry hued, raised and virulent-looking. Blaze turned around and craned to see his back. The wings were definitely his favourite of the marks. They were stylised, and yet incredibly detailed. Somehow the charcoal lines conveyed the sense of vulnerability and power he'd felt when his true wings had sprouted from his back.

That had happened. He was sure it had happened.

Or at least as sure as he was about anything anymore.

Leaving the mirror, Blaze kicked open his bedroom door and picked his way across the piles of debris to the armoire. His mood improved the moment he pulled a fresh black T-shirt over his head. Boots and a leather jacket followed then his hardware; kohl, a flick knife and a pistol. Given how many people were after him, he wasn't taking chances.

Finally, he pulled the vial Vervain had provided from the back pocket of his trousers. It was an ornate little thing, some sort of stone overlaid with filigree. He pulled out the stopper and took a cautious sniff, but there was nothing within.

He was five short minutes away from having his head removed from his shoulders, or some other equally horrid form of demise. The youkai and the Talon were likely scouring the city looking for him, hence doing a five-fingered knuckle shuffle so he could spurt into a jam jar wasn't high on his list of priority activities right now.

Yet, there didn't seem to be any way of avoiding it.

Blaze slumped backwards onto the bed and lifted his feet up, of all the stupid craptastic shit to be faced with. He tugged down his fly and wrapped his palm around his cock. It felt as though he were pumping someone else's. No feeling of pleasure burst over him. He had no sensitivity.

Shit! The stupid tattoo hadn't just stayed his transformation. It had made him fucking impotent.

"Blaze, hurry it up!" Asha's voice echoed up the stairwell.

He was tempted to call her upstairs and tell her to suck him, see if she could coax any life out of it, but for once the image of her on her knees didn't tempt him. Instead, he made a few loud groaning noises and daubed hair wax into the vial. He shook the contents up with some water, and smiled grimly at the result. It looked convincing enough. They'd just have to hope Vervain didn't insist on an authenticity test. Although, who knew what demon seed truly tasted like? He sure as hell didn't.

5. DEATH TOLL

VAST AND MAJESTIC, the cathedral at the heart of the Old City remained the oldest surviving relic of the days when the gods were actually idolized. Now most of the temples were fallen and only a few ancient and exclusive religious sects remained. New gods had found favour among the affluent in the Heights: money and status, washed down with a hearty dose of Blood Rain. Regardless, the cathedral still inspired a sort of quasi-religious fervour. But not today.

The Talon were in disarray, their leader fallen, killed by a boy and one of their own.

His partner.

Him, indirectly.

He should never have allowed Blaze and Asha to escape, but how could he know that act would result in Talon's death? What was to be done now? There was no second in command. Talon's authority had always been absolute. He occupied such a lofty pedestal in their hearts they could hardly comprehend his demise. And yet, it had happened. He'd watched the halberd pierce Talon's chest. Seen him fall, and checked the body.

Jaku pinched the bridge of his nose. Somehow he had to bring this unruly pack of miscreants back under control and make them work together before the youkai gained any ground in the city. Unfortunately, he hadn't even an iota of Talon's power with which to accomplish that. One snap of Talon's fingers and an icy glare were all it would take to line them all up like bowling pins. Mind you, one snap of Talon's fingers could also snap your spine.

Talon had studied the old tongue. He knew how to talk to the world so it sat up and listened. He coaxed it, nurtured it, so that when he asked it to dance, it leapt to do his bidding in the same way his proud demon-hunters did.

"We should hunt and kill the witch and the demon whelp," one of his fellows cried. Jaku didn't bother trying to identify which one. It didn't matter since the sentiment was repeatedly echoed around the ring. He guessed it was unity of sorts. Except, he wasn't sure he wanted them out hunting Asha. What good would it serve? Better they concentrated on their traditional enemy, the one on the cusp of seizing power if all the astronomers and seers were to be believed.

"I agree."

Shit! Talon?

His heart sang with joy, even as terror

knotted up his guts. So, he lived. Jaku ought to have known his master wasn't so easily destroyed.

All the candles in the building blinked out. The cathedral doors blew open and a chill wind rolled up the nave. Jaku coughed and choked as the fingers around his throat squeezed then released. When the lights returned, Talon lounged in his throne, not a mark upon him. At his feet, the pair scheduled for guard duty lay dead at his feet.

As typical Talon's torso was bare, save for a long silver chain, from which a key hung. Lower, a tattoo of thorns girdled his slender hips just above the line of his low riding leather trousers.

"You're alive," someone gasped.

Talon cocked his head, and settled his pale gaze upon the speaker. "How delightfully observant you are, Ouran. A pity none of you are so attentive to what is occurring on the streets. We are on the brink of a new age, and yet there are no guards at the doors, and we have no presence among the people. Tell me, why is that?"

As a group, they all took a united step back from the dais.

"Jaku said you were dead, slain by the youkai whelp."

"As you can see, Jaku was mistaken." The sultry smile that showed just the hint of teeth suggested the issue wasn't entirely finished with. Talon rose from the throne and toed the bodies at his feet, so that they toppled from the dais. "Someone remove them." Several hunters scurried to do his bidding. "The rest of you, arm yourselves, there's a battle to be fought." They scattered, leaving Jaku alone with Talon.

"Now, Jaku." His master's voice entwined itself around his senses, until his skin tingled so much he couldn't help but scratch at it. "The inner sanctum, I think. We have much to discuss."

"Oh, shit. He was done for, and it would not be a quick death like those of the two guards."

Talon's rooms occupied the entirety of the old chapter house, and were the most beautiful and frightening part of the cathedral. A fresco of angels covered the ceiling, and all the walls were clad with wood, that had been carved by master craftsmen into intricate designs of roses and gargoyles. Talon kept the furnishings sparse: two tables full of alchemy equipment, a lectern, and a sumptuous old tester bed, plus a single, vast, circular chair.

Jaku stood and kept his gaze upon the wainscoting. He dared not look at Talon, even though he still loved him every ounce as much as he feared him. His master circled him, then came to a halt resting against the closed door.

"I trust you're going to justify your actions. You knew what you were doing when you aimed at that fiend. You knew it would strike me. The youkai prince runs free now because of you." Talon dropped into the chair and hooked his long legs over the arm. "I should snuff you out of existence, but I find myself strangely moved to spare you."

"I betrayed you," he said, being obstinately honest. It was the best policy with Talon. Screw-up and you'd better admit it, or the consequences tended to be lethal. 'But you betrayed us. You ingested the demon whelps essence." The vision of Talon smeared with Blaze's semen and tears made him want to raise his halberd and charge all over again. Instead, he squeezed his eyes closed and tried to tame his rage. "You sought oneness with him."

"I did not betray you, Jaku. You merely misunderstand my intent. I don't wish to see an era of youkai rule any more than you, but one mustn't outright defy the universe. It expects a demon prince. Therefore we must give it something of that ilk. His essence is a mere a mask. We'll give the world its era of pleasure and perversion, but not one where the youkai rule and feast upon us. Instead, we'll rule and we will enjoy the bounties of this new age.

Jaku risked a glance at his master. Talon's long hair had slipped forward over one eye, and he twisted the key hanging from the chain around his neck idly within his fingers.

"Do you truly believe the boy capable of leading the youkai to dominance? He's barely master of himself. If it weren't for Asha he would still be in your cage."

"Don't be fooled by appearances, Jaku. He may seem a weakling youth at the moment, but he's just a child—a demon child. Once he grows and lays claim to his true title you won't doubt his capacity for destruction. The city will burn. His domain will be comprised of smoke and ash and he will show no mercy to his foes. Fire and agony will mark the full extent of his thousand-year reign."

"Only according to a prophecy that has no serious validation."

A thousand years of raging torment, humans being herded like cattle. Would life under Talon be so very different? Who knew what magic he'd already used to twist his own soul? Silver runes covered most of his skin. Invisible in normal light, they shimmered whenever the candlelight hit them.

Talon steepled his fingers, and tapped them to his chin. "I'm hurt you're even considering that pup as a better option."

The bastard was reading his mind again.

"You're hardly a benevolent lord. Instead of raging fires, what do you offer? Passion that burns cold. Frozen cruelty?"

A quick smile chased across Talon's lips. He swung his legs free of the chair arm and rose. "Have I been cruel to you, Jaku?" He gently lifted Jaku's chin with his fingertips, traced the smooth skin of his upper lip with a thumb. "I guess I have. I've known all along you wanted me, but I've never called for you. Not once."

Jaku held his breath, while heat flared in his groin. Nervously, he glanced at Talon's bare chest. His dark stubby nipples had tightened into points, and he stood with one thumb hooked inside the band of his trousers. Fine-boned, lean and wiry, yet muscles knotted across his abdomen, and where the fine band of golden hairs grew down from around his naval to his loins. He possessed the strength of several of his more muscular demon hunters.

One false move and he could kill me.

He'd never seen Talon completely naked.

When he'd watched him fuck, Talon had kept his trousers on. But, he had seen enough to know the tattoo of thorns that encircled his hips also decorated the length of his cock.

"I saw you die. I checked. I even prodded you to make sure." That he'd also wept and felt his heart fracture he left unsaid. Talon was particularly adept at reading his mind anyway.

Talon eased open the buckle of his belt and slid it slowly through the loops, until it lay flat across his palms. "Crocodile tears. There was murder in your heart when you struck. There still is."

"Then why don't you punish me?"

"Punishing you is what brought us to this point. Punishing you, by ignoring you, that is. Look at me."

Jaku raised his head enough to meet Talon's eyes. Eyes he so often nearly drowned in. They were vivid blue, the corollas a ring as dark as midnight around the edges, but where once the pupils had been inky pools, they were now no longer round, but elongated and feline.

"I'm not risen. I'm reborn, Jaku."

"You're one of them." The words were barely out before Talon leaned forward and captured Jaku's bottom lip between his own, compelling him to stop. He held him there, not so much kissing, but rather commanding him. *Be still. Listen up.*

Jaku didn't move. Even if he'd wanted to, he wasn't sure his muscles would obey. Talon's scent, sweet as honeysuckle and far deadlier than nightshade, ensnared his sense. Talon's taste, subtly metallic, tingled on his tongue.

Talon drew back slightly, breaking the kiss, but still maintaining his hold upon Jaku's arms. "No, I'm not one of them, but nor am I entirely as I was. I understand their cravings. There's an itch beneath my skin that begs to be satisfied. Perhaps more than one itch." He delivered another kiss, this one to the inside of Jaku's wrist, where the veins were thick and ran close to the surface.

Every hair on Jaku's body stood alert.

Talon smiled. "Take off the frippery and the lace. Show me the real you. Don't you get tired of looking like a girl?"

"I don't know." The muscles in his abdomen cramped. Jaku nervously straightened one cuff. No one had seen him naked for a very long time. Even Asha, when she'd dressed past wounds had only ever seen the minimum amount of skin. He didn't care to look at himself unclothed. The truth of his body was too raw. The male lines of it too removed from the image that stared out when he looked in the mirror.

Talon reached out and traced one agile finger over the neckline of Jaku's coat. "Come now." He twisted the top hook, so that it sprang free of the eye, causing the stiff fabric to part. "What exactly is it you fear? How many exquisite layers do I have to peel away before I see the real you?"

"Stop."

Talon popped another hook, and then another.

"Don't." Jaku's toes curled within his boots. He wasn't in any way exposed, a shirt, and three additional layers of fabric lay beneath his gown-like coat. Still, the release of each additional hook stripped a little more of his identity away.

Something snapped inside him. Without warning he lashed out and hit Talon in the face. The impact stung his hand and knocked Talon backwards a pace, but gave him little breathing space.

Talon's pleasant smile vanished, replaced by something infinitely more malicious as his cheek reddened. He bared his teeth. "I'm beginning to think you've a fetish for being flayed."

Jaku dragged in a ragged breath, shocked by his own action. His knuckles ached. He stretched his fingers across his mouth, but there wasn't an apology in him. Hitting Talon felt almost as good as kissing him. The adrenaline surge was certainly the same.

He clenched his fists, dragged them down to his sides, waiting for Talon's retaliation. It wouldn't be kind. Talon caught hold of his chin and turned it, staring Jaku straight in the eyes. Then he began to laugh, a rich bubbling, melodious, and delighted cackle.

"Jaku, you fool." Talon held him trapped in his gaze, then his will was pushing into Jaku's mind, throwing open all the closet doors where he hid his worst deceits and most intimate fantasies. "I'm offering what you've always wanted. You get to take her place. You've wanted to be her all along, did you not?"

"She hated you," he said of Asha, remembering his partner's stricken white face, and the ghosts that chased across her eyes whenever Talon had led her into this private sanctum.

"Detested me with every ounce of her strength, I think you'll find, even as I made her purr with ecstasy. Quite the perfect love affair." Talon's cat's eyes glinted with malice. He turned his back on Jaku and shimmied out of his boots and trousers, revealing a narrow arse and pleasingly long muscled thighs. Unable to help himself, Jaku watched Talon climb onto the bed and sink into the pile of cushions.

"Come." Talon patted the mattress beside me. "Discard the foolishness and join me."

Torn between desire and revulsion, Jaku clenched and released his fists. "How can I? I don't even know what you are. You trained me to kill youkai, not to follow them to bed."

"I am not, and never will be one of them."

Jaku pinched the bridge of his nose as a multitude of conflicting thoughts collided and destroyed his attempted at rationality. He wanted Talon, had done from the first time they met, but he didn't want to climb into bed with a demon, and he couldn't bring himself to peel off his clothes. "I can't undress."

Talon sat up. "Are you that hideous?"

Jaku shook his head. In his mind's eye, he could see them entwined upon the bed, two hard male bodies pressed tightly together, no femininity, no curves, only angles and firm planes of muscle working against one another. It wasn't an image he felt comfortable with. He glanced down at himself: the long skirt of his coat, a slash of neon in the form of a ribbon, thick heavy brocade. Like Asha, he appeared the height of feminine gothic decadence, and that image was comfortable and safe. He'd been playing this role for so long the guise had become second nature. People mistook him for a woman, until he opened his mouth. There was no altering the fact he had a man's voice.

Demure and deadly, he still remembered the words Talon had spoken to him the first time he'd donned the costume, and now his leader was intent on stripping it from him. He'd have to return to what he'd once been, rough and uncouth, a bruised, starveling child, desperate, confused and unloved.

Talon recruited from the streets. There were no interviews, no tests. He didn't employ thugs or psychopaths. He kindled flames that would otherwise have burned out. Jaku had been virtually naked when he'd arrived, a thin shirt over a shredded pair of britches, a woollen hat pulled down over his frostbitten ears, and a cardboard blanket. He thought Talon was an angel.

"Jaku," Talon's voice pierced the memory. "You're not that boy anymore. You're a grown man, and one of my best hunters. Now, come to me. Does it help if I turn off the lights?' The room plunged into darkness, save for a single ball of flames, which hovered by the bedside.

How he longed to extinguish that final light too.

Slowly, Jaku undressed. He tried not to think as he removed every layer, tried not to see himself. Still, humiliation coloured his skin as he stepped from his briefs. He cast them onto the pile of clothing and crawled shamefacedly onto the bed.

"And here we have it. No hideous scars or deformities, just a man with a hard-on." Talon wrapped his hand around Jaku's partial erection, making him jump. They lay stomach-to-stomach, cock-to-cock in the semi-darkness. Talon's breath, light and eager, buffeted his cheek. They didn't kiss, but rolled their hips together instead. Jaku's elaborate braid came undone, and fell in a sheet around his face. Slowly, Talon shimmied downwards, working over Jaku's chest and abdomen to his groin. Jaku couldn't watch. He closed his eyes and focused on the perfect image in his mind, only he couldn't quite hold it intact. It kept fracturing. What Talon was doing felt too goddamn good to imagine as something else. He clung to the sensation of bliss as Talon's tongue tormented his balls.

Jaku laced his fingers into Talon's blond hair and tugged him closer still. He bucked his hips, thrusting deeper without reserve or care, and Talon took it. He revelled in it, even as Jaku's seed rose and spilled.

Spent, Jaku collapsed. Both the sheets and his stomach were shiny with sweat. He knew what was coming when Talon rose over him with a half-crazed gleam in his eyes. There'd be bite marks all over him by tomorrow. He gasped as a canine punctured the skin. They both watched the blood bead in the wound and roll slowly down his abdomen. Talon drew his tongue along the length of the rivulet. "You taste good. I appreciate the gift. Don't fear; it's no new youkai trait I've acquired. I've shared blood with all my lovers."

"Is that what I am?"

Talon bit into his own little finger, and smeared the bright red blood across Jaku's tongue. "I need someone I can trust. A second, if you like. I know you. I know where we stand."

"You think I won't kill you again."

Talon took Jaku's hand in his and sucked the knuckles. His tongue dabbed between Jaku's index and middle fingers. "On the contrary, I know you would." He squeezed Jaku's palm tight, and worked a line of kisses over the back of his palm. "You know there's no return to how things were once this is done."

Knew it. Barely needed to consider it. He'd already sold his soul years before. There'd been hunger in Talon's eyes then, and there was hunger in them now.

Jaku's fingers clenched upon the sheets. He'd wanted this for so long, yet his body protested every inch of the entry. It was heaven and it was hell. The line between discomfort and pleasure blurred a little further with every thrust. He braced himself. Lifted his hips, and surrendered completely to Talon's mastery.

6. EYRIE

**

"The Talon are the guardians of the peace.
We are the protectors of the people.
It is our role to eliminate the youkai who would infiltrate
our homes and consume us in our sleep."
–Talon's indoctrination speech.

**

A SMALL GROUP of locals idled by the base of Eyrie, as Blaze and Asha approached. Men whom Blaze had grown up with here in the Birdcage.

"Blaze?" one of them hollered, apparently pleased to see him, at least until Asha stepped into view.

Although nothing outwardly changed, Blaze wasn't fooled. Years of living here had given him ESP when it came to his associates itching for a rumble. Their attention had shifted from him to her. Demon hunters were a rare and unwelcome presence in the Birdcage. Few of the martial and administrative rules of the council applied here in the heart of the most ancient and rundown part of the Old City. Lawlessness was rife. People picked fights because it was something to do.

"Hey," Blaze replied, walking forward. He flashed the gang a smile, taking careful note of the flick-knives being toyed with half out of sight.

"What are you doing with her, man?"

Having first checked to make sure Asha was facing the other way—her focus was firmly on the ascent ahead—Blaze thrust his hips back and forth in a crude simulation of coitus, resulting in some lewd guffaws from the guys as they slapped each other's backs.

"Always said you had weird taste."

"No weirder than yours."

"Man you're planning a horizontal jig with the Angel of Darkness, nothing out-weirds that."

Sadly, from where Blaze was standing far too many things were weirder than contemplating sex with Asha. Far, far too many things, but he wasn't going to get into that now. He didn't suppose they'd take it too well if he admitted he seemed to be turning into something that snacked on their kind for fun.

"Holler if you need some back up."

"Yeah, I'll do that." He strolled towards the base of the path, guiding Asha ahead of him, while praying the boys stayed put, and didn't decide to use him as a cheap form of entertainment. There'd be a blood bath if word got out that he was attempting to enter the Eyrie. Same as there was every time an attempt was made.

Watching people expire was what passed for meaningful entertainment around here, whether it was as a result of their poor judgement or at a public execution. A form of sadism ran through the city, why else were petty thieves still locked into gibbets? Such punishments had long stopped meaning you'd get pelted with rotten eggs or the remains of someone's kebabs. It was an instant death sentence. The gibbet mightn't kill you, but the Ghost Wind that blew out of the Death Ward every night certainly would. The hungry dead spared no one.

The Ward Breaker already awaited them when they reached the summit. He stood with his arms folded and hood drawn back, beneath the graffiti-riddled stone archway that led onto the plateau. His long robe hung open like a duster coat, beneath which a clingy vest displayed every ridge of his torso. The man was ripped like a pit fighter. Not quite what Blaze had expected from a quasi-priest. Vervain's long legs were covered in some sort of unidentifiable reptilian hide.

"I was beginning to think I'd been stood up. Second thoughts, or did he require help beating it?" he asked Asha.

Eyes as dark as bitumen ensnared Blaze, held him trapped a moment. The corner of Vervain's lip curled, as his gaze narrowed upon the depiction of a crow standing before a red sun painted onto the shoulder of Blaze's jacket.

"Problem?" Blaze asked. He didn't like Vervain's sneering disdain, or the glitter of unshared knowledge lurking in the depths of his unnaturally dark eyes.

Vervain ticked his lips with his long fingers. "And if I do?"

"Save the pompous macho crap for later." Asha stepped between them and thrust the vial and the rest of the payment against the solid ridge of Vervain's chest. "If you need to snarl at each other to find out who's top dog, do it when we're in less of a hurry. Word of our presence here has likely already spread. You have your payment, so just open the door."

Vervain popped the lid of the vial and sniffed. Then put his tongue to the rim.

Shit! He'd realise. Accept it...Accept it.

Vervain sealed the vial and stuffed it into a pocket. "Stand well back." The copse-man cracked his knuckles.

Blaze retreated to the edge of the hexagonal platform, and leaned against one of the quartzite rocks that stuck out from the cliff face like rows of jagged teeth. There was no view to speak of, save of the distant hills. The protruding rocks completely obscured the streets of the Birdcage below.

Couldn't have been much of a watchtower with that view.

His back to one of the teeth, Blaze reservedly returned his attention to Vervain. He'd seen enough spooky dooky hoohah up here for the novelty to have long worn off, but he couldn't deny Vervain was different. Power rolled off him and battered the surroundings like sprays of hail.

Blaze hitched up the collar of his jacket. Most people didn't even get close to the door. Bindweed obscured most of the cliff face. Its criss-crossing lattice of vines made it look like the perfect ladder, but folks had lost more than fingers for attempting that sort of foolishness.

Vervain pressed a single finger to one purple stem. He started a whispering hum; his voice cast so low the hairs on the back of Blaze's neck stood on end. He shuddered. Hell knows what the guy was doing, but the air began to chatter, and the rock beneath Blaze's palm grew warm and throbbed. He broke contact with the stone and crossed his arms. There was something all too familiar about the odd inflections of Vervain's voice, something strangely compelling about the language. Words weren't meant to be so tactile. The warm burr of each and every syllable teased his senses leaving him with a tart yet salty taste in his mouth.

His skin itched.

It seemed the guy was actually genuine.

The bindweed covering the rock face burst into flame, within seconds the purple vines had slithered back from the doors leaving them free for Vervain to touch. The copse-man caressed the rock, coaxed it with the indecipherable words of the old tongue as if it were a lover, until the doors simply rolled back leaving a gaping hole in the mountainside.

"Blaze," Asha called, already darting across the threshold. He followed, but turned back when he realised they were without a light, and that Vervain had paused on the threshold.

"Not curious?" he asked.

Vervain shot him a cold smile. "I'll catch up. I can't walk here without paying respects to the dead of this place first." He covered his head again with his cowl.

"Dead? Asha, wait. This is a tomb. You said it was a watchtower, not a crypt."

She turned, narrow nostrils flared, before her porcelain mask fixed rigidly into place again. "Blaze the entire city is one big necropolis, and right now you've more to fear from the living. Get in here."

He spread his hand in Vervain's direction. "He's—"

"The rules are different for Vervain. He's a

Death Warden. We don't have time for this." Her skirts brushed against his thigh as she reached out and snagged his wrist. "Blaze, let's go."

7. HALL OF ANCIENTS

"I kill demons!" –Asha Lemarche

BLAZE SQUINTED AT the shapes around them. The light was poor, but not entirely absent, though he couldn't detect its source. They appeared to be in a vast hallway formed of stone, not hewn or carved but smooth, as if a hot wire had been drawn through the rock itself. The acoustics reminded him of the cathedral, eerie and echoic. Hairs all over his body stood on end, and his skin prickled.

"Something about this doesn't smell right."

"The only thing I can smell right now is you." Asha gave him a significant look, making it plain she wasn't referring to his armpits, but to the demon miasma he was apparently still giving off.

The path descended down a shallow flight of stone steps into an enormous cavern easily as wide as the city plaza.

"I never realised this place was so big. I thought it'd be just a couple of small rooms."

Asha's skirts swished as they swept across the stone floor. "That just proves how deceptive appearances can be."

How well that observation applied to him. All covered up, as he was now, he looked no different to how he had most of his adult life, yet alien blood stirred in his veins.

"The air's fresh," Asha remarked, leading with her sword drawn.

"Must be air vents, somewhere."

"To go with the light source."

In the farthest corner of the cavern, light bled from the ceiling in a silent cascade. It tumbled, like water over rocks, multihued, full of flashing sparkles that vanished into shadows on the chamber floor.

Blaze turned towards it and felt something tug at the mark on his chest, dragging him forward. He needed to feel that light on his face. His hands scraped against the cold lids as he scurried between rows upon rows of tombs. Until he stood inside the light, basking in the glow.

Beyond the cascade, on the far side of the rainbow, monstrous rope-like tendrils of purple bindweed hung in knots that reached almost to the floor. Blaze drew to a hasty stop, just shy of slicing himself to ribbons. A pair of feet hung level with his nose.'

He looked up. Held within the shadows of the vines, a man hung crucified.

"Asha, get over here."

She arrived in a flurry of skirts virtually the moment he spoke. Where's the danger? her expression asked. Her lips formed a sour pout when she spied the figure hung among the coils of vines.

"It seems the place isn't as impenetrable as you thought. He must have crawled in through the light shaft."

"Maybe." Blaze leapt onto the top of the nearest tomb.

"What are you doing?"

"I'm going to get him down."

Somehow he'd sensed the man's presence in this vast mausoleum, which made him—whoever he was—important. Although, maybe it wasn't the man but something he carried. He wasn't ruling anything out anymore. Not now, not ever.

"We don't have time for this." Asha managed to sound pissed off, exasperated and bored in the same sentence.

Blaze spared her no more than a glance. "I have time for it."

They'd come here looking for information, but the place was so vast they might spend hours, days here and never find anything relevant. This seemed too big a clue to ignore.

He realised the guy hadn't been there long the moment they were face to face. The flesh bore no signs of desiccation nor did the sickly sweet smell of decay assail his nostrils. Blaze dubiously poked him with one finger, only thinking about it the split second before he made contact. Thankfully nothing more than the resistance of cold flesh met his touch. He lifted his hand higher, cautiously twisted it between the vines and into the man's clothing trying to reach the pulse point in his neck.

More cold, flesh greeted him, along with the

faint but unmistakable flicker of life. He snatched his hand back fast, tearing open the back of his fist in the process. "Shit!" Blaze licked at the wound, and eyed the man again, wondering if he'd imagined that pulse.

Asha grasped his hand, but immediately dismissed the wound as a scratch. "Are you finished now? What are you going to gain by releasing him, besides razored hands?"

"He's alive."

"What?"

"He's alive. We have to help him down."

She shook her head slowly. "The hell he is. He's not our problem, Blaze. We don't have time for corpses."

The hell he wasn't their problem. He wasn't going to leave anybody to die, stranger or otherwise. "Help me," he growled. "Because he is alive, and I do have time for this."

Blaze drew the flick knife he'd picked up from home and sawed at the thorny stem holding the man's right arm aloft. It wasn't easy given that one false move and he was likely to lose an arm.

He'd not mentioned it to Asha, but he'd packed a more effective weapon in addition to the knife, the cold metal of which weighed heavily in his jacket pocket. "Asha, please!"

She sheathed her sword and climbed up beside him, nimble as a fox, and twice as dainty. "I'll take his weight, you worry about the vines."

The first few cuts weren't too much trouble, but each further slice dulled his blade, until he was sawing at each stem and blood trickled from his nicked fingertips down between his digits, to compromise his grip.

"I need another knife,"

"Stick with that one; we're going to need all the weapons we've got. Besides, you're nearly there. Just apply a bit of pressure."

"If I apply any more pressure, I'm likely to end up in there with him."

"Then come down and let him hang."

Incensed by her lack of compassion, Blaze slashed at the last of the vines. They gave, and the guy dropped. Asha tottered under the sudden weight. "Blaze!" she cursed. He caught the guy's arms, but Asha stumbled throwing them all off balance. Blaze sat down heavily, and the comatose man flopped into his lap.

His hair was the black of a winter's night, knotted and entwined with razor sharp thorns, but still shone with the lustre of spun silk. The faint shadow of stubble darkened his upper lip and the tip of his chin. The fuzz combined with the hollows under his cheekbones to make him look gaunt. Although, given the bulk of his shoulders, and the hint of muscle beneath his slashed clothing, such a sallow and diminished state seemed unlikely to be the norm.

"Still think he's worth the effort?" Asha righted herself. She helped support the man so Blaze could shimmy out from beneath him. Safely back on his feet, Blaze rubbed a hand over his aching rear. "It wouldn't have been right to leave him there." Besides, now he had a good look at him, he was even more intrigued.

Asha joined in rubbing his butt, sending him into a frantic jig of escape. Any contact between them right now was too dangerous. He couldn't risk her getting too close and realising that damn sigil she'd branded him with had rendered him impotent. If she did, she might grasp that he'd duped Vervain.

"Don't," he complained. Regardless of the intimacy issue, her actions were a fraction sadistic, considering, within an hour or two he'd be sporting a contusion the colour of Hades.

She looked at him, a trifle glassy-eyed and then shrugged as if the rejection didn't matter.

It did matter. It took all his goddamned strength.

Blaze returned his attention to the man. Long tendrils of bindweed still entwined his torso, the lancet-like thorns wedged deep into the flesh. Blaze tried covering his hand with his cuff and tugging, but only succeeded in re-opening the cuts on his fingertips. He sucked at them, and gave Asha his best pleading look, envying her leather gloves.

Gloves, he should have picked some of them up from home, too. Damned if hindsight wasn't glorious.

"It's probably not worth the effort. He's unlikely to survive." Asha slipped her hand into the pocket of the guy's torn shirt.

"Hey." Blaze made a grab for her wrist, but she already had the man's wallet in her hand. He withdrew slowly, as she flipped it open and drew out the I.D card.

"Given that the last stray I picked up turned out to be dangerous, I like to know who I'm dealing with." She stared pointedly at him, her green eyes ablaze. Him. Yeah, okay, he got it. Maybe it would have been better if she'd left him where she found him.

Blaze took the ID card from her. He had to spit and scrub at the dried blood to make out the name. "Raven. I can't make out the second bit."

Asha shook her head. "It's not important."

His skin prickled at the dismissal. He knew the Talon were notorious for their disassociation with all those around them. Being nicknamed dolls wasn't entirely down to their appearance. It was also a statement about the apparent emptiness of their souls. They were automatons, unfeeling, cold to the core. Except... "You helped me, why not him?"

"I kill demons, Blaze. You were being attacked by them when we first met."

"But, after that? You'd done your job then."

She sighed so that her thick eyelashes dusted her cheeks as she lowered her gaze. "There's no riddle to it, Blaze. I fully intended to walk away and leave you. I would have done, but Jaku's always had a thing about pretty blonds. He said you were too cute to leave for the ghouls. You should thank him for your rescue, not me."

So, her former partner had saved him, not her. He chewed that morsel over as he drew his flick knife again and tried to lever it under the vines. Did it change anything? Not really. The upshot remained the same. He'd been escorted back to the cathedral and locked in a cage—a cage from which Asha had then helped him escape.

Why she'd helped him he'd love to know. Needless to say he didn't think compassion had driven her. That she had issues with Talon had been obvious just from observing them for the five minutes he'd see them together.

Maybe he was just the excuse she'd needed.

And he guessed he was a good bargaining chip should Talon come seeking to reclaim his property.

"There'll be nothing left of his arm if you keep that up."

"So, help," he snarled, allowing his frayed emotions to get the better of him.

Asha lifted her shoulders in an eloquent shrug. "If I must." She tore off the remains of the guy's shirt, wrapped it around her gloved fist, then grasped one end of the vine. With a swift jerk she ripped it free of the skin.

The man sat bolt upright. He blinked and his mouth opened around a silent scream before he sagged away again in a dead faint.

"Worked, didn't it?" she retorted, before Blaze had a chance to complain. She untwisted the tattered shirt from her hand and dropped it to the ground.

An elaborate tattoo of a large black bird covered the entirety of the man's right side, extending over his ribs and his bicep as one continuous pattern. "Raven," Blaze assumed. The bird looked as if it had been shot in the chest due to the bindweed lacerations. In addition, several long welts striped the guy's stomach.

"Whip marks," Asha said when he pointed them out. "Painful, but they'll heal up."

"Know that from experience?"

To his astonishment she laughed.

"Talon never left lasting marks. He's far too precise for that. Besides, welts such as these would spoil his belief in perfect body aesthetics."

"Don't you have any of your beetle dung left

you can feed him?" Blaze asked, knowing she had all manner of things secreted about her person.

Her brow creased almost imperceptibly.

"That resin stuff you fed me when you found me after the first youkai attack. The painkillers."

"Blaze, he needs to be awake for that. You have to chew it. Besides, what I have, I'm not wasting. Things were different when I picked you up. There was a plentiful supply awaiting me back home. You're my priority, not him."

"Then at least help me get his wounds covered up." She might not be a doctor, but she'd already proved she knew a darned sight more about field surgery than he did. Hardly a surprise, given she'd spent years hunting demons through the streets.

Asha reached into one of her many hidden pockets and extracted a small tin, which she threw at him.

Blaze caught it.

"Rub some of that on him. It might help, or it might just sting like hell. Either way, don't bother me with this again unless he wakes up. Then, I'll be interested to hear exactly how he got in here, and if your goddamned fascination is justified." She turned away from the plinth. "I'm going to look around."

"Maybe he's a ward breaker like Vervain," Blaze called to her retreating back.

She gave a derisive snort. "No dabbler could unravel that lock, and if he was more than that I'd have heard of him. Be careful, Blaze. You can never tell when something's going to bite you in the arse."

8: CONNECTIONS

ASHA MOVED BRISKLY, putting as much distance between her, Blaze and the stranger as she could. She didn't like it, she didn't like it one bit. How exactly had he got into this supposedly impenetrable tomb? The only other ward breaker in the city with the knowledge and skill to force an entry the way Vervain had done was Talon. And there was no reason for him to be in here ahead of them.

No, there was definitely something suspicious going on. She didn't like the way Blaze had honed in on that fool as if they had a date. And while an element of the erratic coloured most of Blaze's actions, she dared not dismiss that fact.

Answers—they needed answers. She had to focus on their purpose in coming here and block out the distractions until later. There had to be a way to neutralise Blaze and keep him safe. She'd thought the tattoo would be enough, but then Vervain had sown the seeds of doubt.

Doubts she didn't need. There were already too many unknowns. She needed some solid facts to prop up her theories, although the likelihood of finding them here looked increasingly poor. There were plenty of carved depictions of youkai-demons and humans decorating the walls of the vast chamber, but the illustrations were far too open to interpretation.

Not far from where they'd entered she found a picture of the Blood Moon.

Asha touched the faded carving. In some places coloured pigments still clung to the stone. The perhaps once-brilliant red had now faded to a dull ox-brown. This appeared to be the end panel of a sequence of five related images. Five pictures...five stages to his coming? Kell's Prophecy spoke of the Burning Prince and how there would be several stages to his ascent. She searched the images for some sort of reference point, a hint that something she'd witnessed had already come to pass, but nothing stood out.

Nothing obvious anyway.

Blaze remained hunched over the man he'd found. She could make out the top of his head on the far side of the chamber. He seemed safe enough, so she refocused her attention on the reliefs.

In one scene corpses lay heaped in the roads and blood ran freely through the streets. In another, fire raged. A single, winged figure hung in the air above the flames. Was the figure their destroyer or their saviour? Was this the future or the past? Did it matter? Talon had always maintained time was circular, and what had happened once would inevitably happen again.

"Fascinating, aren't they? Scholars could spend many lifetimes interpreting them." A warm hand settled upon her shoulder. Asha turned to find Vervain smiling down at her from the depths of his hood. His black eyes glittered like the hoar frost.

She pointed at the fiery panel. "Instigator, saviour, survivor or merely an observer?"

Vervain shook his head. "That's the problem with prophecies. You can only truly interpret them after the fact, once all the pieces have fallen neatly into place. Anything I say would be pure guess, and a far from educated one."

"Then I can't stop him changing and wreaking destruction upon us. Look at him, he's innocent. There's no anger in him. Am I supposed to stand back and watch him change? What the hell sort of event is it going to take to make him into a destroyer?"

"Who says that's what he'll become?"

"You identified him by that mark, claimed it was of the royal house. The prophecy says he'll destroy us."

"Are you sure that's what it says, or is that your interpretation? No—" Vervain reached beneath his hood to rub at his shorn scalp. Mirth danced upon his lips and in his eyes "—it's not even your interpretation, but Talon's. Still, trusting his word, Asha? Because I have to say, if there's going to be a paradise of perversity on Earth, my money would be on Talon being behind it, not your fledgling prince."

"Leave Talon out of this." She turned away

from him, anger tightening her fists. He had a point though. Hell, Talon had said as much himself about usurping control.

Talon would never bow to the youkai, no matter the cost.

"Are you saying I should abandon Blaze to his fate? That there's no point in attempting to avoid it because we don't know what the outcome will be?"

"Youkai rule is inevitable. There will always be times when they are ascendant and we are in decline, but that doesn't mean it is imminent."

She turned back to face him, incredulous. "We know their ascent is linked to the Blood Moon, and the astronomers all say it is about to rise."

"True, but I prefer to see that rise as a window of opportunity, a time of instability and flux, when change may occur but isn't inevitable. Possibility, Asha. Not pre-destiny." He sighed. "I don't doubt Blaze is likely their Prince reborn. He bears the royal mark, but, consider also that he has no more power at the moment than you or I. He has no army, no generals, and no direction. All he amounts to is potential. He could acquire all those things and bend this city to his will, but equally, he could fade back into the obscurity that birthed him, or you could stop him."

She dug her teeth into the plump flesh of her lower lip as she chewed over Vervain's words. Really he was only telling her what she already knew. That ultimately, she had to trust her own instincts to lead her along the right path.

"You believe I should kill him, end it now."

Vervain gently touched her cheek. "If only it were that simple, eh?"

Asha stepped away from the caress. "I could do it."

The Death Warden just smiled and ever so slightly shook his head. He turned away and began perusing the frescos. "Not without killing yourself in the process," he whispered, so low she suspected he almost intended her not to catch it.

She grabbed his wrist, spun him to face her. Surprisingly, he came without any resistance. "Explain."

"I can sense energy lines connecting you two. The more time you spend with him the stronger they'll get, until it's impossible to separate yourself from him. You already feel more for him than you should."

Asha curled her hand as if by doing so she could hide the brand on her palm, the mirror of the royal mark upon Blaze's chest. Hell knows, if she were going to kill Blaze, maybe she ought to kill herself too, since they were both branded. Although she was pretty sure hers was only a mark of association.

"It would have been better for us all if you'd left him for the Ghost Wind," Vervain remarked. "At least it would have been a swift and merciful death."

Asha released his wrist. "Do you rank seer among your titles now, too? I never told you how we met."

"Don't be a fool, Asha. I know what goes on outside my own gate."

She stared back across the dingy chamber at Blaze. His blond hair shone, flecked with golden tones from the light stream. His expression showed both compassion and kindness as he rubbed the ointment she'd given him into the stranger's wounds.

She'd slaughtered folks she'd known all her life because they'd turned out to be something other than what they seemed. Yet she'd allowed Blaze to live.

Why? Because she couldn't accept he was the enemy.

The youkai were deceitful and cruel. Her role was that of executioner, not reformer. Maybe she ought to end it now. Catch him off guard as he leant over his patient, except a nagging doubt turned her gaze to the faded wall carvings again. Perhaps Vervain was right, and she couldn't kill him.

"The connection between you and Blaze grows stronger." Vervain's voice washed over her like a soothing balm, no longer suggestive or insinuating. He spoke fact, nothing more. "The thicker you allow it to become the harder it'll be to sever."

"It would serve no purpose to sever it now. That might do more harm than good." The youkai were a violent race. Maybe violence, like sex, would trigger an unwanted reaction.

Vervain's brows knit together. He squinted across the chamber at Blaze. "Energy lines connect him to his patient even as we speak."

"And are there energy lines connecting you to him?"

Vervain drew his hood forward, so that his expression slid entirely into the shadows again.

He didn't reply. After an uncomfortable pause, he turned his attention back to the wall.

Asha followed suit. "What do you make of this?" she asked when enough silence had passed to realise the topic of Blaze was, at least for the moment, done.

"Try it."

Asha hesitated with her hand held aloft over the curious depression in the wall. There was no tingle of power emanating from it, no itch tickling her palm.

Vervain crowded her expectantly. "Frightened it'll summon a dragon?"

"A fucking enormous demon with bad breath and attitude actually."

Vervain chuckled. "You should be so lucky."

Okay, what the hell. You only lived once. She filled the impression with her palm. For a moment nothing happened, then the rumble of stones grinding against one another reverberated up her arm. Asha pulled away fast as one of the huge stone slabs swung as if hinged. Flames flickered into life in the gloom beyond, shedding light on a narrow winding staircase guarded by two grotesque stone masks, but it was the burning sensation on the back of her neck that made Asha pause.

Vervain stood directly behind her. "Shall we ascend?"

She couldn't think of a single good reason to refuse.

9. RAVEN

**

"So they set their dead to rest in the Hall of Ancients."
–Enchanter's Nightshade, Tales of the Old City.
**

GROGGY AND PHOTOSENSITIVE, Raven Idriss tentatively opened his left eye. Hell knows where he was, and whatever he was lying on was so cold his knackers were in danger of freezing. For a moment, his vision swam. Then a jarringly familiar face moved into his field of vision. Blond hair, those molten expressive eyes, a smile that could reduce even the most sexually inured to orgasm. He'd been saved.

Finally.

He tried to rise, only for his muscles to protest and his saviour to gently push him back down again. "You're hurt. Lie still a moment. The bindweed's made a complete mess of your arms and trunk."

Raven relaxed, surprised by how comforting he found his saviour's touch. Chipped, black-painted fingernails pressed to his brow. He half-heartedly shook his head. How many times now had he woken to this vision? His dehydrated brain was playing tricks again. He blinked; trying to clear the film from his eye, under no doubt that he was still incarcerated in the Hall of Ancients. When blinking didn't help, he tried raising an arm. Fiery streamers of pain tore through the muscles, forcing him to relax.

The smiling vision leant over him again, closer this time, as if examining him. "I'm Blaze, by the way," it said. "You're Raven, right?"

Dreaming. Definitely, one hundred percent dreaming. No doubt about it.

"Is your other eye okay? Can't you open it?"

His right eye had never been okay, at least not in a normal vision, increased depth perception kind of way. Still, he supposed it wouldn't hurt to see what it made of this phantasm. He fluttered the lid a few times, before fully opening the eye and letting the rose-coloured tint it gave everything settle over his environs. For once, Blaze didn't blink out of existence.

Shit! He sat bolt upright. Never mind the pain, or the fact that his heart was racing as though the Ghost Wind was at his back.

"Hey, you've different coloured eyes." Blaze leaned in far too close and squinted as if trying to properly assess the colour.

Normally, Raven would have growled over the invasion of his space. He didn't care for intrusive souls, but this wasn't a normal situation, far from it.

"Yeah," he replied. There wasn't really a lot else to say. "One grey and one amethyst. And yours are copper."

Blaze jerked away from him so fast one would

think he'd been scalded. He glared; perfect Cupid's bow lips pursed in outrage. Fear shone in the inky depths of those copper-coloured eyes.

"They're blue. My eyes are blue, not copper-coloured."

Raven looked at him again. Were they blue? He tried closing his right eye. Blaze's irises still glowed like molten copper, forming two of the most beautiful eyes he'd ever seen. "My mistake," he apologised. "It must be the light."

Lie accepted. Blaze's shoulders slumped. He took a tentative step forward again, so that he stood level with the foot of the sarcophagus on which Raven was perched. "Guess you're still a bit muddled. Must have been down here a while, eh?"

Raven eased himself into a more comfortable sitting position, and took stock of his surroundings. Fuck, if he wasn't still stuck in this arsehole of a tomb. As far as punishments went, this one sucked big time. Question was, had Blaze come to break him out, or was his time up? Nar, couldn't be, else the twins would have come for him.

Of course, Blaze being here, meant things were afoot.

"Yes, a while," he agreed.

Environs assessed, he turned his attention to his protesting body. His arms were a mess of puncture wounds and deep scratches that itched liked hell, and his chest wasn't much better. A pot of bilious green ointment sat balanced upon his thigh, alongside the remains of his shirt. He poked a finger into the pot then brought it to his nose and sniffed dubiously. Smelled like day old fish that someone had tried to mask the scent of with pine fragranced air freshener. Worse still, the stuff was smeared all over him.

"You were lucky we found you," Blaze said.

As there was no discernible "we" about based on a quick scan, he assumed Blaze's companions were outside.

"How'd you get in here?"

Raven slid off the tomb and onto his feet. First opportunity and he was getting himself a shower. A nice long, hot, steam-curling, soul-warming shower, but first he needed to do something about these wounds.

"I'm not really sure," he replied, feeding Blaze yet another lie, not wanting to get into the whys and wherefores of his punishment until he knew exactly what was what with the world.

He stretched his arms above his head, attempting to ease out some of the niggling aches, only for pain to tear through his right bicep. His arms dropped like a stack of overbalanced logs. Tentatively, he reached across and squeezed the muscle. There had to be a thorn still in there, and by the feel of it, wedged pretty deep.

"Here, let me help."

A strong hand curled around his arm. Blaze eyed the wound carefully.

"I can just see the tip of it." He scratched at the thorn with his fingernails. "It's coming. Keep still. Ah, there... nearly... Yes, got it."

Blaze held up the inch long barb, which curved like a sabre-tooth and was sharp enough to cut through rhino hide.

A thick rivulet of blood ran down Raven's arm. He grabbed the remains of his shirt and pressed it to the wound. He looked like a man who'd been locked in an iron maiden for a fortnight. The reality was, that might have been preferable.

Blaze continued to peer at him as though he had two heads.

"Something up?"

"Déjà vu." Blaze shook his head. "Weird." He dropped the tooth-like barb, tried to catch it, and managed to slice open his index finger. Blood immediately pooled in the cut.

Raven reached out to him, meaning only to apply pressure to the wound, but somehow ended up with Blaze's finger in his mouth. Ah, bliss... the scent of him, the taste of his blood, intoxicating, overwhelming. A few drops and desire plumped his loins. There was no mistaking his liege. His blood roiled with potency, fire flowed through his veins, and infected Raven's senses. The blood in his stomach writhed like tumbling smoke curls, and he sucked harder, wanting, needing more.

His wounds began to knit, slowly at first, and then more noticeably as new skin stretched over the old.

Blaze snatched his hand away, and wrapped his bloodied fingers in the hem of his T-shirt. "What are you doing?"

Still high on the taste of him, Raven leaned forward. He wanted nothing more than to grab his sovereign and deep kiss him in the traditional youkai way, but a single pace in his direction sent Blaze scuttling backwards among the tombs. Fear made the coppery hue of his eyes burn brighter.

"What are you? Who are you?" he demanded.

"I'm sorry. I didn't mean to alarm you." Raven

reached out a hand, but Blaze continued to back up.

"You've healed," he said, biting his lips.

The last of the wounds in Raven's arms closed. "Ah, yes," he remarked. "So I have."

10. FIGHT AND FLIGHT

THERE WAS SOMETHING wrong with the sky. Asha stood with Vervain on the octagonal platform that formed the true pinnacle of the Eyrie. It was as if someone had increased the contrast between the firmament and the city skyline. A malingering sense of unease permeated the air too, causing goosebumps to break out across her skin.

"Can you feel it?"

Vervain moved to the edge of the platform and peered over the carved quartzite balustrade. "I feel it. Not in the heavens, though, but down there on the streets." His cowled head turned, so his gaze took in the city's vast panorama, from the distant gargantuan towers of the Heights which shone in the sunlight, to the bleak claustrophobic hovels of the Birdcage below.

"What is it?" she asked, even though she

wasn't expecting a straight answer. Her old partner, Jaku, had always said Vervain acted like he'd swallowed an oracle for breakfast and a pit fighter for lunch. An image, she had to agree, Vervain lived up to.

"Vervain?"

"The city screams," he muttered, and followed the observation with a shrug.

"The city—what? Wait!" She eased her sword free of its scabbard, the horrid prickle of unease becoming increasingly pronounced. "Are the youkai amassing? Is the Blood Moon about to rise?"

"I don't know. Listen."

At first she heard nothing save the distant hum of ordinary citizens going about their everyday tasks. Then it started. The murderous peal of the cathedral bells. "Youkai! Youkai!" the huge bass bell seemed to cry. Its message soon topped by the cry of the trebles, "*Fight. Fight. Fight. Fight. Fight.*"

Asha ran to the opposite side of the platform and stretched over the wall in the direction of the cathedral. "Why? The main threat is not here yet. Why call everyone to war?"

"A pre-emptive strike." Within the depths of his hood Vervain's dark eyes took on the appearance of scalding slate.

"We have to get Blaze to safety."

"There is no safe place left on Earth for you to take him."

"There has to be somewhere." She scurried back towards the winding stairs that led into the cliff-side.

Vervain shook his head. "If you want him to live, you may need to make the youkai your allies."

"No!" She turned abruptly. "No, he's not one of them. He doesn't want to associate with them. Besides, the youkai are not the dead, Vervain. You can't bargain with them, because their word means shit. We're just playthings to them—food. They won't listen. They'll just attack, and rend and tear, and feast. And if Talon drives them onto the streets with this call to arms there'll be a blood bath."

She'd seen cornered youkai attack. She'd seen the remains of half-devoured captives. Even Blaze, before she'd marked him, had been driven crazy by his need for flesh and blood. He'd contented himself with sex, but in truth when he'd pinned her down, she hadn't really known whether he was about to fuck her, feast on her flesh, or both.

"Blaze is different to the rest," she muttered, trying to maintain her confidence in the assertion.

"You're not wrong. He's their damn prince."

"I'm marked too, Vervain. What does that make me?"

His eyes narrowed, but there was no time to respond. A soft *thunk* sounded behind her, and she turned her head in time to see a second winged demon swoop towards them.

Asha raised her sword. The battle had begun.

BLAZE CAUTIOUSLY BACKED away from Raven. The feeling he'd been here, done this before with this man, was simply too strong to shake off.

I know him.

He knew it on a gut level, and yet they'd only just met. Disturbed by the notion, he continued to stare at Raven, watching his wounds knit, until there was nothing left to see of the many puncture wounds that had covered his body.

"What do you want?" He kept sliding backwards between the lines of stone boxes, towards the entrance where he'd last seen Asha. "Who are you?"

"Raven is my name, and I think you know what I am."

He knew, but his mind didn't want to accept it, and Asha had never explicitly stated how to spot a youkai in human form. Hell knows, maybe it was his blood that had caused the guy to heal. He'd healed from wounds that should have taken months to fix before Asha had that damn doodle drawn on his abs. The thing was; Raven didn't seem remotely perturbed by his sudden health. He'd accepted it as if both being injured and instant healing were a normal occurrence. And what had that weird finger-sucking, blood-licking thing been about? Were the two things even connected?

"Stay away from me."

Maybe he ought to call Asha, let her deal with this. She'd specifically asked him to holler when Raven woke. Problem was, just the suggestion that the guy might be youkai would likely see her lopping his head off as a precautionary measure, and Blaze wanted some answers first.

"Stay back. Stop there and answer me. Why are you here, what do you want with me?"

"You put me here as a punishment. Don't you recall?"

"Punishment? Why would I punish you? I don't even know you. I've never been in here before."

The gleam in Raven's mismatched eyes said otherwise. "You have known me, Blaze. Forgive me, but how much time has passed that you don't remember? What happened?"

Blaze refused to hear him. He covered his ears and yelled for Asha; as if making a noise would void the certainty he felt deep in his heart, that what Raven swore was true. They did know one another.

Tiny, split second fragments of a past he didn't remember fell like splintered glass through his brain. Places Blaze couldn't remember, occasions that had no meaning to him, but in all of them Raven stood a little to his right, covering his back.

"I'm Blaze Makaresh. I'm twenty-three years old. I was adopted from an orphanage by my grandmother when I was eighteen months old, after she found out about the death of my parents. I've lived with her all my life, here, at the base of this rock, in the Birdcage, until she died four months ago.

Raven didn't say a word, but Blaze bore the distinct impression he was reciting an entirely different, and much longer, biography. After a significant pause, during which Asha failed to appear, Raven slowly cocked his head to one side. "What date is it?"

"I don't know. What does it matter?"

"How long until the Blood Moon rises?"

"Why? Why do you need to know that?"

"Because my senses tell me it's no more than a week away, and you're—well, you're not exactly yourself."

"I'm fine." Blaze slapped his hand down hard on the top of the nearest tomb. It didn't matter that it was an outrageous lie. Raven didn't need to know anything about him, and yet he was torn. Letting his guard down might get him some straight answers, but equally it might get him killed. "Asha!" he bellowed again.

This time, the sound of footsteps quickly followed. His fists tightly clasped, a wave of relief nevertheless coursed through his tightened muscles. A tick beat in his jaw as he anticipated her appearance and prayed she'd analyse the situation before she struck.

A black-clad figure appeared, but it wasn't Asha. He cried for her again, then the screaming started inside his skull and he lost his voice. Blaze dropped like a stone. On his knees and temporarily blind, he swayed, hands clasped to his head. Pain raced across his scalp and seared the nerve-endings. His shoulders were alive with flames. It felt as if razor blades were scoring his skin, the pain so sharp he simply had to endure until he was left numb.

Still the ear-splitting sound of voices penetrated his skull, called to him, caressed him and then shook him as if he were nothing more than a baby's rattle. Blaze jerked, pulled by invisible strings, before his mind gave way to oblivion.

W HAT WAS THIS *song that made him want to weep?* Raven cursed as Blaze crumpled and collapsed at his feet, whimpering and tearing at his hair and ears. The strange call tugged at his senses too, brushed against his skin like a warm sirocco and determinedly tacked across his body until his skin began to split.

Someone was forcing the change. How, he didn't know, though he'd heard such things were possible. Normally, shifting form was a voluntary affair. Raven spun on the heels of his boots, but failed to pinpoint the source.

"Show yourself." His voice pierced the gloom, the notes higher and sharper than they ought to be.

Nothing... Just a breeze-like whisper and the continuation of that horrid song.

Resisting the pain that started in his cerebellum and lanced down his spine, Raven bent to comfort Blaze. The boy was burning up. Sweat glistened across his temples, and ran in small rivulets across his face and down the sides of his neck. Silently screaming, Blaze's hands clasped and unclasped. He tore at his hair, his T-shirt, and finally at the flesh below.

Raven goggled at the sliver of exposed flesh. Charcoal lines spiralled around Blaze's navel in a complex criss-crossing pattern, among which shadows clawed at the bars of their ink-drawn cage.

"Shit!" No wonder he wasn't right. Who in hellish eternity had inflicted such a mark upon him? The muscles of his own stomach clenched in horror at the binding.

Lunacy, sheer lunacy.

Only a complete sadist would do such a thing. Those marks would tear him apart.

The sound of footsteps snagged his attention. The Talon! He should have realised. Three of them swept down the steps into the Chamber of Ancients, their black garb fluttering around them like wisps of smoke. Nice to see they were still the same crazy dichotomy they'd always been. Shame their outward beauty never seemed to mask the malice in their hearts. Cold killers, that's what they were, motivated by bitterness and not much else.

Weapons drawn, the first two hunters rushed towards him, white-painted faces alive with hatred, while the third hung back, his fingertips pressed together to form a steepled arch, as he concentrated on the complex rhythm of the hellish chant that was about to tear Blaze apart.

Damnation, where were Blaze's friends? They needed back up right now. Although, he was beginning to suspect those friends were imaginary. Gently, he released Blaze onto the floor. His liege's eyes had rolled back into his skull, and while his screams were entirely internal, Raven could nevertheless still hear them. They formed a second stream of agony entwined around the chant that tugged at his own sinews.

He had no choice. He simply couldn't resist.

At least it was quick. The skin along his spine ripped open and black wings fanned from his back. His nails extended into the sharp claws. Raven rose to meet the Talon attack.

The problem with the Talon was they expected to win. All they ever encountered were foot soldiers and hapless wanderers, which meant they were cocky and too assured of success. That gave him an opening.

Faster. Stronger. Raven swooped under the blurred arches of their swords and punched upwards with his claws, perforating the chest cavity of one and the stomach, and likely the spleen of the other. Stunned, the first guy dropped his weapon and clasped his hands to his wounds, before his legs gave out. Raven seized the demon-hunter's sword, and dragged it swiftly across the other man's throat. He too fell, which just left the contralto to deal with.

The man had his eyes closed in concentration. He opened them abruptly as Raven loomed before him. His words faltered as Raven scored a line across his brow. Blood seeped into the wound, and trickled down over the singer's brows, leaving him half-blind. Desperate, he drew his weapon. Suddenly enjoying himself, Raven danced out of reach. It had been too long since he'd enjoyed such freedom to let rip. He skipped about a while avoiding the crazed swings of the hunter, testing out his reflexes and working the stiffness out of his joints. Then, when he'd had enough, it was simply a matter of slash and puncture.

He fell on the singer's fallen body, and tore a piece out of the man's shoulder. He licked at the blood covering his face. It had been too long. Far too long, and his stomach growled in hunger. But he hadn't forgotten Blaze.

Still smeared with blood, Raven crawled over to where Blaze lay comatose. Carefully, he pushed up Blaze's shirt and studied the charcoal swirls of the tattoo. This time his liege had survived, but there was no way of telling if he'd do so again.

"I'm sorry, but I swear you'll thank me for this later." He ripped through the flesh of Blaze's abdomen as deep as the muscle in two directions, and then skewed the pattern, bent to the wounds and licked them clean. It was obvious the action had worked when seconds later the skin began to knit, and perhaps not a moment too soon.

Raven relaxed back into his human form.

Blaze yawned and stirred. He sat up. "What happened?" His eyes narrowed. "Were you licking me?"

"The Talon attacked," Raven replied, neatly bypassing the second question. He rose up again sharply as another black blur sped towards them.

"Stop!" Blaze rose between him and the figure. "Asha, what happened?" Fine spots of blood covered her porcelain-white face.

"Run," she demanded. "We're found; both the Talon and the youkai are here for us."

"To where?"

Vervain appeared behind her. He glanced at the bodies of the demon-hunters on the floor and gave Raven a grudging nod. "We'll figure the details as we go. Run."

11. WISHT WAY

THEY SPRINTED DOWN from the Eyrie with only the wind in pursuit; the cathedral bells still chiming out their angry warning. Blaze ran at the centre of the group, the others having formed a protective ring around him. Asha led, with Raven at his right flank and the Death Warden on the left. Blaze sensed their terror; it zipped through the air around them and chafed his skin, but he didn't share it. Instead, exhilaration fired his senses. Gone was the discomfort of the last few minutes, the awkward tension between him and Raven, and the gnawing pain that had so recently savaged his body. Elevated, alive, and most importantly, free, he ran, enjoying the rapid thud of his pulse and the cruel nip of the easterly wind.

Something had changed, the threatening shadows no longer held quite the same fear. He almost relished their approach. *Bring it on*, he wanted to shout. *Bring it on...I can handle it.*

Raven... Raven had done something to him. He glanced at his companion whose dark hair was caught in a thick topknot that swished and swayed as he ran. There remained something jarringly familiar about him, the rigid tilt of his jaw and those oddly mismatched eyes, but as much as Blaze scoured his past he couldn't latch onto a single distinct memory of them being together, just shades and impressions. Not enough to risk his life upon, but no reason to dismiss him out of hand either. He wished there was time to stop and find out what Raven had been doing up there in the Eyrie. Really find out, that was, not just be given some brush off answer about him having locked Raven in Eyrie as punishment. That didn't make sense. He'd never set foot in the place before today. Well, not in this lifetime at any rate, and he wasn't at all sure he even believed in multiple existences.

And in any case, that answer made no sense. If he'd been responsible for Raven's incarceration, why did the guy seem do darned pleased to see him, and why had he leapt to his aid when the Talon attacked? If he'd been left tied up with bindweed somewhere, he was damned sure he wouldn't be defending the perpetrator against anything. No, he'd be laying on a few additional kicks of his own.

Nothing... Nothing made sense anymore. He snatched another glance at Raven.

Hell knows what this was all about, or if he'd ever find out. But he'd seen enough of those bodies before they fled to realise that all questions aside, he felt safer for having Raven around. The man knew how to handle himself. Asha was lethal, but she couldn't handle the entire might of the Talon and the youkai all at once. Not alone anyway. And he didn't want to think too hard about whether she had plans to play them off against one another. Any action on that scale would turn things into a bloody massacre, and no way did he want to be responsible for that. This place was his home. He'd grown up around these people.

Then again, maybe it was already too late. Maybe that's what fate had already decreed and all he could really do was keep pace with the rushing tide of events.

The gang that had been loitering at the base of the Eyrie were gone, as was every other sign of life. The thing about the Birdcage was that it was always teeming with life. This might be the unloved heart of the city, squalid, decrepit and riddled with vermin, but the Birdcage never slept. It was never still, never this quiet.

He drew to an uneasy halt, forcing the copseman to a sharp stop behind him. Above an open doorway a sign creaked as it swung in the wind. Besides that, not so much as a beetle moved. Even the scavenger rats that squabbled over human waste were absent.

"Where have they all gone?"

Asha twitched. Her black finery rustled as she turned to assess each of the five alleyways that lead out of the area, the sound unnaturally loud in the echoing silence.

Vervain answered, "More importantly, you

might ask, why have they gone? The locals aren't normally so afeared of the Talon, only of—"

"—the dead," Asha said.

"I was going to say of each other. Twilight is hours away. The dead don't walk abroad in daylight." Vervain drew his robe tightly about himself again, so that it shrouded his craggy features as it had done when they'd first been introduced. "Don't fear over that. The dearly departed are safely confined behind the Lich Gate, as they should be."

"What is it then? And where do we go?" Blaze asked.

Vervain gave a quick shake of his head, so that the ghosts trapped within the weft of his grey robe reared and snarled. "That I can't answer. This isn't my fight."

Mocking laughter burst from Asha's throat. "It's as much your fight as ours, copse-man, or have you forgotten the demon blood splattered across your robe and the new rents torn through the shoulders? You're stuck in the middle of this dead zone with whatever is prowling, just the same as we are."

"That doesn't commit me to a side."

"Oh, doesn't it? Then how about the alchemical signature that you've left emblazoned across the top of the Eyrie? Talon will know you aided us. He'll read it in the ether. He has no patience for fence sitters, Vervain. His concept of sides is altogether black and white. With him or against him."

"I've duties to attend to, or are you suggesting I shirk them?"

They glared at one another. Asha's brow

furrowed infinitesimally, her hand closed around the hilt of her sword.

Vervain's black gaze turned as bleak as a mid-winter sky.

"If the dead start prowling, you'll have more to fear than the rising of the moon and the fate of your youkai lover. You presume too much, Asha Lemarche. I may negotiate for you, but we are not on the same side. I'm not on anybody's side. The only reason I'm still here is because your partner hasn't paid me yet." Vervain's gaze shifted briefly to Blaze.

He had known. Blaze's gut clenched tight. The only surprising part was that he'd waited this long to mention it, when he could have simply refused to open the Eyrie door.

Asha expression remained unchanged. Maybe she'd suspected him too? But weirdly neither of them asked him why he'd faked the payment.

"Save this." Raven stepped between them. "We need to leave here. Whatever is out there has likely caught our scent by now. Arguing amongst ourselves is only shortening the odds on our capture."

In a whisper of steel against the sheath, Asha released an inch of her sword. The green of her irises seemed unnaturally bright as she turned her attention to Raven. "I don't recall inviting your opinion. Who are you, anyway? By rights you should barely be able to move. Not so long ago you looked more like a pincushion than a man, and yet I'm not seeing any wounds."

"Asha," Blaze reached towards her and brushed his fingertips across the back of her hand. "He helped us back there. They'd have had me if it wasn't for him. That song... It was agony... tugging me in all directions."

To his chagrin, his explanation only further soured her expression. "You took out Adrick and the others single-handedly?" She glanced at Blaze. "You didn't help?" Blaze shook his head and she freed another three inches of blade. "Start talking," she spat at Raven.

"Asha, please!" Blaze pleaded.

She pushed him behind her.

"I heal quickly, that's all." Raven raised his hands in surrender. "I'm ward-marked. I'm sure you know all about that. You're one of the Talon, and he's said to be a master of the art."

"There are no marks on your skin besides the Raven tattoo."

Raven glanced sidelong at Blaze, before slowly moistening his lips to reply. "You didn't strip me. They're well hidden, but get us someplace safe and I'll show you."

"Here." Sword now entirely free of the sheath, Asha raised the tip, ready to lunge.

"Come on." Raven glanced warily round at the still eerily quiet streets. The wind howled around them and nipped at their clothing. Blaze edged around from behind Asha's back. If there were ward-marks on Raven's skin, he wanted to see them. Their presence would certainly explain a few things. Tentatively, the other man slid his fingers inside his waistband, and popped the button with his thumb. The thick muscles of his shoulders flexed as he bent slightly.

"Wait!" Vervain pushed aside Asha's sword. "Listen."

"The bells have stopped," she said after a

moment's pause. "Talon's rethought his devilry. It doesn't change anything."

"No, ignore the bells." Vervain turned his sharp gaze upon Raven, his brows drawn tight. "Dogs... I can hear dogs barking. You heard them before. That's what you were trying to say."

Raven barely inclined his head.

"What's that smell?" Blaze raised his hand, but there was no keeping the ghastly stench from his nostrils. In fact it seemed to permeate every pore so that it stuck to the skin. "Yueww! Worse than the bogs at the Iron Horseman after the Martyr's Day wrestling."

"I've smelled month old corpse less pungent," Vervain agreed. He turned a full circle, seeking the source of the stench.

Blaze followed his three hundred and sixty degree turn. "Yeah, but what is it? You said the dead didn't walk in the daylight."

"They don't. Nor do they cry like that."

"Something living smells that bad? Man, it reeks."

"Run!" Asha's yell rent the air, putting an end to their pained grimaces, and the tension between them.

"What?" Blaze took a step towards her, but she swung both her sword and its scabbard wide, warding him off.

"Run. Take him and get out of here," she barked at Vervain, although it was Raven who acted. He grabbed Blaze's arm, half tugged, and half shoved him in the direction of her brief nod. "To the left. Up Twitcher's Parade and onto Hangover Street. Don't wait for me. Just go. We can regroup at Maggot's."

"But what is it?" Blaze yelled, as Raven bullied him into a sprint. He might not feel as dead on his feet as he had an hour ago, but he couldn't match Raven's pure physical strength encouraging him up the hillside. The guy didn't give an inch, not even a quarter. He dragged him, virtually carried him in a bone-crushing grip into the cobbled alleyway. "What are they?"

"Wisht Hound," the other man murmured.

"Leave now!" Asha screamed.

From the corner of his eye, Blaze saw the first of the beasts bound towards her, as large as a calf, but with the jaws of a tiger. Its long canines were already stained with blood. That one glimpse was enough to freeze him. The chill struck him deep in his chest. Blaze's heart squeezed tight, and then began to thud at twice normal pace. He half-turned, ready to run back to her, except Raven wouldn't let go. He stood there, immobile as a mountain, while the lolloping beast raised its head and bayed. Its deep, hollow moan was the cry of a thousand lost and desperate souls, wretched and pitiful and so wrought with pain, tears spilled unbidden down Blaze's cheeks. Five other hounds bounded into the square from the direction of his home.

Raven wept too.

Asha's face was deathly pale.

The lead dog pounced and the scene before him dissolved...

BLAZE STOOD IN his grandmother's room, her best china smashed across the floor, already littered with her nightgowns. The dried remains of her half century old wedding posy lay strewn across the bedspread like spots of coloured paper. Black shadows flitted on the periphery of his vision. A sliver of black ribbon floated down to rest across the pointed toe of his boots. "Grandma," he called, even though he knew she'd left him. "Where are you? What's going on?"

Somehow he stood on the landing outside his room, though he didn't remember climbing the stairs. In the hall mirror he saw her reflection, smiling, beatific, her skin as papery soft as the old flower petals.

"You shouldn't be here, Blaze. Not now. Not at this moment."

"I heard you calling, and they've wrecked all your things."

"Earthly possessions." She made a phft sound and gave a dismissive flick of her lace shrouded wrist. "They're meaningless to me now. You were the only thing that really mattered. But it's not time yet. The transformation's not complete. You need to find your third. Nothing can happen without it. Nothing."

"Third what?" If only he had the faintest clue what she was talking about. What the hell did he have two of that required a third? "Why didn't you tell me what I was...and better prepare me?"

"I don't make the rules, Blaze. I just played my part, and now you have to play yours. You have to leave here. They're coming for you. They have your scent." He looked around, but the house stood silent. In the distance he could hear the vague rumble of traffic on the street. There was nobody here but him, and no apprehensive flutter of nerves in his stomach warning him of danger.

"You have to leave now!"

Her pale face vanished from the mirror, leaving him staring at his reflection, blond hair swept backwards into spikes, and the corolla of his blue eyes glowing copper. He had a bruise on his temple, presumably where he'd hit the floor when the Talon had attacked, but even as he watched, it yellowed and faded.

Third what? Who's coming? Talon perhaps. The youkai—whoever it was that was in charge of them. Maybe he ought to just pick a side and give himself up, and then at least he might have a clearer idea of what was going on.

A single black rune appeared on his cheek, like someone had brushed it on in ink. Blaze spread his fingers to touch it, only for it to glow softly around the edges and then dissolve into his skin. He stared at the spot where the mark had been, waiting for something to happen, but nothing did. He didn't feel any different, didn't grow horns or sprout wings, nothing jumped out and leapt on him. A knot of apprehension tightened in his innards. Something about this wasn't right. Everyone kept screaming danger at him but it was all quiet. Peaceful, actually. So tranquil, he felt like lying down on his bed and closing his eyes for some well-earned rest.

He stretched and his stomach growled. The skin across his abdomen felt curiously tight, like tears had dried upon the flesh. Blaze's hand strayed towards the tattoo. He lifted the hem of the shirt, and stared at the design. Even looking at the reflection, the alteration was obvious. Somehow the design had been skewed so that the lines no longer fit together in the same way but formed a jagged S-shape instead. He traced the pattern with a fingertip. Raven... Raven had been licking him when he'd come round earlier. Somehow he'd altered the design while he'd been out, but why, and how had he made it heal up so fast?

Blaze shrugged off the obvious explanation, refusing to acknowledge the truth about himself or the other man.

Asha wouldn't like it. She'd been trying to help when she'd had him inked. Now the design was damaged it wouldn't work... or would it? Fact was he had no bloody idea.

Asha—the memory of her prompted two curious reactions, first his libido sparked so that he was pleasantly buzzy, thinking of her lily-white skin and those long leather boots that were virtually sprayed onto her calves. Secondly, he realised she wasn't there. She'd told him to run, but he hadn't done it. He'd watched that thing come towards her and pounce. So how had he got here? And where was she?

The moment he recalled the danger they'd been in, a shadow reared up behind him and grabbed him by the shoulders. It spun him so fast it took a few seconds for his brain to catch up with the fact that he'd moved. His arm shot upwards, and caught whatever it was by the throat. "Blaze," it managed to croak, and he relaxed.

He stared at Raven, who had him backed into

a doorway of a steep, cobbled street. The bigger man rubbed his throat. He had blood smeared around his lips and a hunk of gore stuck to his temple. "You back?" he asked.

Blaze nodded, his voice refused to work. Instead, he stared. There was no sign of Asha or Vervain, or the dogs that had come for them, although he could still hear their cries in the distance.

"Where are we? How'd we get here? Where's Asha?"

"Hm," Raven grunted. "Don't ask until you're ready to hear it." Raven gave him a look that made him shut his mouth fast. He'd need those answers soon, but okay, not quite yet. It'd keep until they were somewhere safer, where they could sit down and talk it over in a civilized fashion. Not that he felt remotely civilized, and Raven sure as hell didn't look it. His right eye glowed like a gas lantern, lilac and amethyst at the centre with a golden halo around the rim. There was no pupil to speak of, and hence no reflection of his image, although he could see in the grey eye that he too was blood splattered.

Blaze tentatively reached up and flicked the piece of gristle from Raven's brow. He opened his mouth to ask where it had come from, then thought better of it.

"Think your feet are working?" Raven asked.

He nodded.

"Good. We're not far from Maggot's, but you're a heavy bugger for all that there's nothing to you. We need to run. Try not to look around, just concentrate on the destination, and whatever you do. Don't stop."

"What about Asha?"

"She's following." Raven tugged him out of the nook by the arm, while cautiously looking around. "Okay now? Run. You take the lead, and I'll watch your arse."

THE HOUND SLAMMED into her at chest height, throwing her backwards. Asha landed with a thump. Her dress padded the impact, but not enough to prevent pain ricocheting up her spine and splicing her senses so that she both saw and tasted the bruises forming. The tang of rusted iron filled her mouth, while an explosion of blue forget-me-nots sprang up in her field of vision. *Damn!* Even the resulting adrenaline rush didn't make her quick enough to gain her feet before the beast was on her, plate-like front paws planted on her chest and its horrible gaping maw complete with the worst doggy breath in history right in her face.

Her palm was sweaty inside her gloves, but she still had her sword, even if it was heavy and unwieldy in this position. Regardless, she caught the dog a good one across the side. It didn't budge, just growled in her face and then licked up the side of her jaw.

Its companions ran circles around them. Out of the corner of her eye, she saw them catch a scent and whip off in the directions she'd sent Blaze.

Dammit, no!

The hound's rough tongue caressed her flesh, leaving behind stinging pinpricks of pain that dissolved into numbness. Fuck! The chill ran down her neck and into her shoulder, almost immediately freezing up the joint so she was forced to drop the sword. She stretched the other arm, reaching for the knife holstered around her thigh. *Let's see how this thing liked a blade in its belly.* She'd just bunched up her skirt and got her hand around the knife hilt when a shadow appeared over her, and then the dog rolled sideways, yelping.

Vervain leaned over her holding a large iron frying pan. He offered her a hand up. Asha scrambled onto her feet just as the dog sprang out of its roll. It lurched towards them again, snarling. Vervain struck it across the muzzle, and it dropped again. This time it didn't get up.

"How badly did it get you?" he asked.

Still somewhat off balance, Asha scooped up her sword without bothering to reply. Pins and needles threaded down her left side, making sheathing her sword an absolute bitch of a coordination feat. But, she did it. A grimace contorting her black painted lips, she shuffled determinedly over to the felled hound and gave it a damned good kick.

"I'll take that as a 'not too bad', shall I?" Vervain's shadow joined hers over the prone hound.

"It's not dead."

"No." Vervain clapped the base of the iron skillet against his palm. "But at least it's off our heels for the moment. I'd offer to oblige, but it'd be messy, and it'd be hell to get out of the threads."

She snuck a sidewards glance at him. At some

point in the last few minutes he'd slipped the bottom few buttons of his robe open again, so he was showing a good portion of thigh in addition to the strange grey cloth. From there her gaze strayed to his hand fastened around the shaft of the pan.

"It's not stylish," she remarked. Hell if this darned dog didn't smell like a fish market sewer. Never mind Vervain's clothes, she didn't want to stand around breathing in whatever noxious gas this thing was giving off.

She covered her mouth and nose with the cuff of her dress. "What is it, anyway? Not youkai."

"A Wisht Hound, I think." Vervain also toed it with his boot. On the dog's hind, level with the base of its tail, lay a strange eye-like branding.

She shook her head, not even familiar with the name. "Magic? Talon?"

The youkai hardly needed to summon an animal for the purpose of sniffing them out, since they could detect a drop of spilled human blood from half a mile away. Although she guessed that particular talent was only useful if the person you were after was actually bleeding. Considering how much grief one Wisht Hound had caused her, there was a good chance Blaze was doing exactly that.

Blaze wasn't exactly battle seasoned, and she certainly didn't trust Raven and whatever motivation he had for hanging around to keep Blaze safe.

Four to one odds—they were probably tearing him to shreds.

"Come on." She slapped Vervain across the back, urging him into motion as she propelled herself forward. Unfortunately, her limbs weren't working quite as well as they ought as the hellish venom continued to strike matches throughout them.

Vervain caught her arm and steadied her. "Are you sure you can run?"

Damned if she would stand still 'til this wore off, not with a ghastly image of the hounds gnawing on the gristly bits of Blaze's body flitting through her head. "I'll manage. It'll wear off faster if I'm moving."

Vervain held her steady as she plodded forward, her gait awkward. Still, after a few yards she was moving independently, if in an ungainly fashion.

It became clear after only a few minutes, that while Vervain was certainly handy in a fight, he didn't do much running on a regular basis. Even with pins and needles crackling down her left side, she was soon outstripping him. By the time they were climbing the summit of Twitcher's Parade, he'd dropped back several feet, and the exertion had worked most of the paralysis from her limbs, leastways until she stopped moving. Stationary was another matter. Her skin crawled as though an entire hornets' nest had taken up residence in each limb.

She stumbled over to where the street formed a staggered junction with Hart's Lane and Hangover Street. "Damned in hell!" Pretty much all other mental functioning shut down in protest at the sight before her.

Vervain climbed the last five yards to the brow of the hill, with his hands clutched to his thighs. Slowly, he straightened, still gasping.

Then he exhaled as if every particle of air had been forcefully expelled from his lungs.

"I see I'm going to be very busy tonight. Very busy." He shook his head, and then folded himself inside the cocoon of his robe. "What have you started, Asha?"

"Me?" She glared at him. How could he think—how could he *believe* her actions were responsible for this?

The street before them ran red. Bodies, two or three deep littered the cobbles like rotten veg discarded after market day. A thick cloud of Blood Rain hung at waist height, obscuring the far end of the street. They'd have to wade right through the coppery fog, stepping on hell knows what as they inhaled it to get to the rendezvous point.

Asha carefully breathed through her mouth, trying to avoid the pungent stench of iron and fresh meat. Equally carefully, she swallowed, but it didn't remove the sickly taste from her mouth.

What if they were already too late?

There had to be damn near a hundred bodies down there, and Blaze could be one of them.

She'd told him to run and she'd sent him to his death.

"Retribution?" Vervain asked. "Is he making a point? Talon, you murderous bastard?" He shook his fist.

"They were in the way," she said quietly. "Talon rang the bell, called everyone to arms." That it would result in a massacre had always been inevitable. She couldn't even pretend this was the work of someone else. Not that Talon was personally responsible. He left most of the dog work to his minions. Still, the neatness of the cuts spoke of cold, calculating cruelty, and defined this as the work of her former brothers-in-arms as clearly as if they'd branded the Talon insignia across the forehead of each corpse.

See them as they truly are, not as they appear to you now. Hadn't that always been Talon's teaching? His doctrine? The way he'd made murder palatable. And if sometimes they got it wrong. *Well, not to worry, you'd do better next time.*

Forget the glassy eyed fallen youths and their shocked families. Get over the outrage and abandon fear of retaliation. No one ever fought back. No one questioned them. The Talon were the guardians of the peace—truth, justice, saviours. The Talon kept them safe from the youkai. The Talon were debauched, murdering liars, or at least their master was. There was no hiding that fact after this.

Asha swept her gaze over the piles of tangled limbs, not allowing herself to linger on any one individual long enough to take in the true horror of the scene. Her heart surged with relief every time a flash of blond hair failed to reconnect her with Blaze.

"Do you think they've reached Maggot's?" she asked, barely aware she'd spoken aloud.

"Who knows what's beyond that cloud? One thing, I'm not seeing is any dogs."

12. BLOOD FLOW

"The hunger of the dead is eternal.
The hunger of a demon fades into dust.
That humans see fit to ingest such dust defies understanding."
-Vesper Canon. Conspiracies et Demonica, Chapter 7.

BLAZE WAS HALFWAY along Hangover Street, running with imaginary blinkers on, not looking at anything beside the end of his own nose, when the first body skittered across the cobbles towards him. He stopped abruptly and stared down at it. Brown, lifeless eyes stared back. A huge gash scored the man's torso, and he was entirely missing his left forearm. "What in hell?"

"I told you not to look." Raven grabbed him by the seat of his pants and jerked him forward, over the corpse and the crimson cobbles, straight into the path of an overturned baker's cart and the gaping maw of one of the hellborn dogs they'd been trying to outrun.

"Shitindamnation!" Blaze struggled in Raven's grip, which his companion thankfully relinquished.

Blaze eased back a step, surprised Raven

hadn't commented. "What do we do?" He hit the solid wall of muscle that was Raven's back. Blaze threw a glance over his shoulder and wished he hadn't. Seemed they had company on two fronts, and not of the variety he felt obliged to invite in for tea and scones.

The Talon—two of them—stood before Raven, weapons drawn, draped in their typical black finery with a whole haberdasher's load of lacy frou-frou billowing gracefully about them in the wind. Clouds of coppery dust hung over their heads like rusted halos.

"What do you want?" Raven growled.

"Give us the boy."

"He's mine. What are you offering for him?" Raven eased Blaze out from behind his back and slung an arm around his shoulders. In doing so, he also turned them slightly, so they could keep an eye on both the Talon and the dogs. "Your pet poodles?"

This was it, the running was over. He was about to be dragged back to Talon HQ, mauled and spat on by their egomaniac of a leader. Assuming they didn't just opt for the slice off his head and deliver him in bits option. Where was Asha? Had she already been rounded up?

"Hand him over and maybe you'll get to keep your soul," the taller of the two dolls demanded.

Raven's smile spread across his face like ripples across a pond. "Doll, you wouldn't even know where to look for it."

Did demons have souls?

'Course they did. Damn, he was letting his thoughts get the better of him. He'd been deliberately squishing this stuff to deal with later, like sometime when his mind could handle it and he wasn't being given the evil eye by a dog the size of a motorbike and two of Talon's butchers.

Not that he could really pretend he didn't know that his current guardian angel had demon blood running through his veins, not when he was painfully aware of Raven's temperature, due to the arm embracing his back. Considering the only thing covering Raven's skin was the huge raven tattooed across his chest, he was ridiculously warm to the touch, and growing warmer. Another few degrees and you'd be able to fry eggs on his washboard abs just as if they were a griddle plate.

Youkai. The blood flowing through those centrally heated veins called to him. He couldn't pretend he wasn't feeling the pull of kinship, nor could he deny that his true nature was running dangerously close to the surface again. The metallic smell of blood around him had his mouth watering and his heart skipping with excitement rather than filling him with the urge to retch.

Blaze felt the nervous twitch of his companion's arms.

The guy had sliced and diced three hunters up on the Eyrie. That surely gave them even odds on this one.

Blaze clenched a fist, and was surprised by the adrenaline-fuelled growl of content he felt in his stomach. It was a damn shame he'd blunted his flick knife freeing Raven from the bindweed. He'd have welcomed its solid comfort in his palm right now.

"Last chance to make me an offer or walk away," Raven said.

Blaze swore the demon hunters were cackling like demented banshees beneath their impassive facades, as it was they barely twitched an eyebrow between them before they'd both launched themselves at Raven.

Boy, did the guy move fast.

Still, he also had the dog snapping at his heels as he swung the sword he'd commandeered off one of his previous Talon victims. Blaze planted a foot in the beast's ribs. He may as well have kicked a boulder. The impact reverberated back up his leg and threatened to dislocate his hip, but at least it gave Raven a momentary respite from its snapping jaws.

Beside him, Raven grunted. Metal clashed. He wove and twisted. Then lunged. One of the hunters swayed, arterial blood spraying from his neck, and toppled backwards over the dog. Blaze watched the other demon hunter sag to his knees before bits of cranium hit him in the face and temporarily deprived him of his sight.

Raven grabbed him and shoved him into the doorway of a shop three doors down from their actual destination. "In here."

The doorbell tinkled as Raven swept him inside. Blaze stumbled, and slammed into the delicatessens' centrally positioned table, sending various pots of fish roe and perfumed dainties skidding onto the floor.

"Fuck!" He hammered his fist against the table. To hell with the shattered pots and the nightmare outside that his brain outright refused to process. Why did everyone want an effing piece of him?

He swung round to face Raven. "Who the fucking hell are you?"

Raven had slammed the door behind them and swept all three bolts into place. He stood with his back plastered against the wood. He held one arm clamped across his stomach. "Shush!" he growled through gritted teeth.

Tentatively, Raven peeled away his arm from the skin revealing a knife wound right across his stomach. He made a noise low in his throat as the blood started to weep afresh.

Blaze inched forward a little. "Is it true, what you told Asha? Because if you're ward-marked how come it's not closing up?"

Raven made another noise, this one more of a snarl than a groan. The utterance was almost instantaneously echoed on the other side of the door. The hell hound had wasted no time pursuing them. All that separated them was two inches of solid wood and a few metal pins.

"You know perfectly well how it works, and it has fuck all to do with inked-on squiggles. I need blood...or meat. You know this. You taught me."

Your blood. Your flesh, being the extension of the remark.

Blaze ignored the implication. It didn't matter how many times Raven swore it; he had no memory, well, no real memories of their friendship. The odd glimpse snatched from behind a veil of mirrors didn't count. He walked around the table, pulling out drawers and eventually stumbled upon some cloth napkins. He thrust a wad of them at Raven.

"It'll be okay. Give it a minute and it'll stop."

"Not sure we have a minute." Right on cue the

hound hurled itself at the outside of the door, hard enough to temporarily knock Raven away from the security of the wood.

"Let me look at it." Blaze clasped the pad of napkins, and urged Raven's arm away from his stomach. It wasn't good. The cut was deep and straight. He needed Asha with her needle and thread.

"Lick me."

"What?"

"Like I licked you earlier."

"You did what!"

Who was he kidding? He knew perfectly well Raven had been licking him. Actually, the thought gave him a curious thrill that ran right through his body and culminated in his balls.

"Do it. The flesh will seal." Raven's gaze rolled up towards the ceiling. He jerked again as the dog thumped the outside. "The door won't hold forever, Blaze, nor will my legs."

Blaze looked at the wound again, then up at Raven's face. The other man's skin had leached of colour and the flesh across his temples seemed clammy. Not thinking too hard about it, he dropped to his knees.

"This'll fix it, right?" Blaze tentatively stuck out his tongue and licked at one corner of the wound. There was no helping getting a mouthful of blood for his trouble. Only instead of revulsion, the red stuff hit his tongue and he couldn't swallow fast enough. Wow! He just wanted to stay here, drinking Raven down and enjoying the wave of delirium that flowed out from each of his pleasure centres. The blood tasted... Nah, it wasn't really a taste, more of a sensation, kind of tingly well-being with an erotic twist. The later bit wasn't helped by Raven threading his fingers through the spikes of his hair.

"I have to get you someplace you're gonna get your memory back." He gave Blaze a wan smile. The wound had closed although it was still pink and waxy along the edges.

Blaze rose to his feet and edged back a fraction from the big man whilst wiping his mouth. His balance was a little unsteady, as if he were punch drunk.

Raven reached out for his hand. "Please, my liege."

"What did I punish you for?" Blaze asked. Although the question seemed to have popped out of nowhere, it had been bothering him ever since Raven had first mentioned he'd been locked in the Eyrie at Blaze's behest. That and he had to start considering this stuff if he had any chance of keeping his head.

"Aw, we don't need to get into that now, do we?" Raven flashed him one of his magnificent grins, the sort Blaze was pretty sure melted ladies' panties. To his horror, he began to reciprocate the smile.

"I want to know." He bit down hard and fixed his mouth in a rigid line.

"Blaze."

Blaze looked him right in the eyes and held his ground. Some things one had to keep pressing for, and this was clearly important, otherwise Raven wouldn't have been acting so shady over it.

Glass shattered to his right. They both raised their arms as one hound, then another came crashing through the shop window.

"Dammit! Later."

He released Raven from his gaze and sought out the pistol in his pocket. Crazy he hadn't thought of using it until now. Too late—he barely had a hold of it before the foremost dog leapt straight for him.

Pain ripped through the curiously blissful wave he'd been floating on from ingesting Raven's blood. Adrenaline surged through his veins as the creatures long canines punctured his jacket and entered his flesh. A scream tore free of his throat, his lungs sustaining the cry even while he flailed trying to break the beast's hold. He kicked, trying to sweep its back legs, and when that didn't work he hit it between the eyes with the gun butt.

Damn beast held on, its jaws locked so tight he swore his bones would snap.

A flutter of skirts alerted them to Asha's arrival. She swooped through the broken window on the heels of one of the hounds.

"Asha!" Blaze screamed. Only the sound of his voice didn't seem to stop. It echoed around inside his head until that hurt more than the blasted dog bite. Everything was going black again. The skin across his shoulder blades began to rip. "No!" he cried, realising what was coming. It couldn't happen. Not while Asha was here. He had to stay in control and maintain a human guise. He needed her support. He couldn't lose her, not now, and he didn't want to explain about the tattoo until he understood who and what Raven was.

Suddenly Raven was at his side, guiding his hand, squeezing his finger over the trigger. The loud clap seemed to freeze everyone for a second, and then the hound made one last whimper and slumped, dragging him to the floor with its massive weight. With aid he managed to pry the jaws open and free his arm. Raven surreptitiously sniffed the wounds while Asha's attention fixed on the remaining hounds.

"Poison," he whispered.

Blaze grasped his wounded arm. "It feels cold."

A further shadow filled the broken window as Vervain joined the little group too late to be of aid in the fight. The last hound fell at Asha's feet, its hot innards spilling from the gash across its belly.

In the stillness that followed, the four of them warily eyed one another, while Vervain's shadow carpeted the stone floor. It wouldn't be long until sundown. Nobody seemed keen to make the first move. Blaze dared not release the tension in his jaw for fear of transforming into his demon form. He couldn't feel his right arm, though his brain told him it should hurt like hell.

Raven began rubbing his back. Slowly the ripping sensation across his shoulder blades eased and then faded away.

Finally, Asha sheathed her sword. "Best we move on immediately." Her pale, perfect face turned to Blaze, showing a flash of tenderness that vanished on observing the contact between him and Raven.

"Does your back hurt?"

"It's nothing." Blaze brushed off Raven's caresses.

"Good." Asha inclined her head to the rear of the shop. "Above ground is too dangerous. We can head down into the catacombs below the city from here."

That's why she'd directed them to Maggot's. But perhaps the tunnels and sewers would be safer. It seemed reasonable to suppose the massacre they'd seen on Hangover Street was duplicated in other sites around the Old City.

Using Raven as leverage, Blaze hauled himself upright.

"Keep moving it. The numbness wears off," Asha moved in close to inspect the bite before ushering them all through the door into the rear of the shop. "Vervain, you take the lead."

"For a while," the copse-man muttered. "I've duties to attend to. They'll need my services tonight."

Blaze bit his lip expecting a repeat of their earlier argument but none came. He guessed the swell of new souls seeking the comfort of the Death Ward tipped the balance over Vervain's plans to leave them.

The shop connected to Maggot's, their original destination, via a cobbled alleyway at the rear that also housed the refuse sacks and an old outdoor privy. Maggot's itself remained as it had always been—cluttered and reeking of potions. The skeletal remains of a huge bird of prey hung from the ceiling, and every shelf and surface was covered with row upon row of stoppered glass vessels containing coloured liquids. A weed-filled fish tank stood mid-way along one shelf, and an athanor at the end of another.

"Wait up a minute." Vervain had them catch their breath.

The shop front was boarded up; the place had

been abandoned for months, and as far as Blaze could tell was now a convenient respite point for fugitives. He'd been here twice since meeting Asha, and numerous times before that with his grandmother, in the days when it was still a viable business. He'd often wondered what happened to Old Maggot.

"Did he die?" he asked.

"Who?"

"The owner."

"Yeah, something like that. Heart attack." Asha's attention fastened upon Vervain as if daring him to contradict.

While Vervain rifled among the bottles, Blaze slumped against the pitted table in the centre of the room. Memories of the first time he'd lain with Asha, here in this room came flooding back. He'd been desperate to escape, and equally desperate to have her. Jaku her partner had been asleep on the sacks in the corner. As Blaze pressed his nose to the wood grain, he could almost catch the scent of Asha's body.

There were spots of dried blood on the floor and several of the work surfaces. He watched Raven surreptitiously wet his finger and taste one or two of them. The lantern flame in his right eye sparkled a little in apparent recognition of the flavours.

No doubt he'd caught a taste of Blaze's blood, spilt when sex had sparked his first change. This was where he'd first gained his wings. It was a miracle he'd actually survived. If there'd been a little more space for Jaku to swing his glaive at the time maybe he wouldn't have.

Asha came up behind him and stroked a hand

up his spine from his waistband to his neck. Blaze tensed. He couldn't relax even when she leaned forward and rested her head between his shoulder blades. She wouldn't understand about the damage to the tattoo, which meant for a while at least, he had to make sure she didn't find out. She wanted him to be normal, to be human like her, but little by little he was accepting that wasn't the case.

He had a past he knew nothing about and a future that was equally uncertain.

"I didn't expect to be back here again so soon," she whispered.

"We're running around in circles."

"Yeah."

He sensed, rather than felt, the brief brush of her lips.

Oh, hell. She shouldn't have done that. Because now he wanted her. Right here and now, where they'd first given into mutual desire, and he didn't give a flying fig if they had an audience, or that another wave of attackers might crash through the boarded-up window at any moment. He wanted to hitch up those ridiculous voluminous skirts of hers and plant his palms on the lily-white perfection of her inner thighs, right above her stocking tops. And he wanted to inhale her scent and stick out his tongue, lick and drink, cover himself with her scent. Hold on to her until there were no gaps between them. Envelop her completely until they were irrevocably bound.

That was a new one. He'd never wanted to be close to any of his previous lovers, but equally none of them had ever grabbed him in the guts quite the way Asha did.

Asha drifted away from him, but Blaze held his position, the ache in his loins having rendered him hard and far too eager. He wanted to fuck her and... And other things, that he clamped a lid on. Things that weren't reasonable human behaviour, stuff he could hardly expect anyone to willingly consent to. Well... His gaze drifted towards Raven, but then who was he kidding even imagining for a minute that he was a decent model for human behaviour?

Next quiet moment they got together he was having the truth of that punishment out of Raven. He might not remember dishing it out, but he was damn sure he was going to learn what it had been for. Hell knows, maybe it had been for eating humans.

Asha returned to his side holding a vial of blue liquid. "Vervain's dug this out. Let me have another look at that bite."

"It's fine."

"Get real, Blaze. Damn dog nearly snapped your arm in two."

"Besides," Vervain came to back her up. "This'll deal with the poison, too. We need you up and moving."

"I got this far." He sighed and shrugged his shoulders. Leastways he shrugged the left. He couldn't actually feel the right. Reluctantly, he peeled back the sleeve of his jacket, exposing the puncture wounds. Vervain held his hand while Asha poured the liquid. It reminded him of treacle running down his arm, viscous but icy rather than sticky. The chemical fizzed on contact with blood and left the wounds smoking.

Now he understood why Vervain had grabbed

hold of his hand. He winced and bit his tongue, while a whole litany of expletives echoed inside his skull. *Fuck, that hurt!*

Over Vervain's shoulder his eyes met Raven's.

"I could have seen to those," the youkai male's expression said. Blaze heard the words as clearly as if they'd been spoken. "It would have been a whole lot pleasanter, too."

"Maybe, but also harder to explain."

"She already knows what you are."

"Yes, but not what you've done. She won't like that."

"You let her ink you? You're a freaking fool—my liege." Raven inclined his head a fraction.

"Ow! Get the hell off me. That's enough." Having tugged his arm—which he most definitely could feel—free of Vervain's grasp, Blaze pulled down his sleeve. It looked as if his second best jacket was headed the way of the first. How come Asha's clothes never seemed to get wrecked, but his always did?

Graceful as ever, she swept towards the door, her long skirt a black shadow around her ankles. "Bring some of that stuff with us, Vervain. We might need it later."

The copse-man bowed his head a fraction in acknowledgement. Blaze scowled at the possibility of having to face future icy burns. He'd been beaten and chewed on enough for one lifetime. Okay, perhaps not entirely. There were a few things that still tickled his fancy, although they were all to do with pleasure-related pains rather than plain ol' pain-related pains.

Asha held the door to the catacombs, and to his astonishment, she leaned over and kissed him as he passed. It was the merest brushing of their lips but it cooked his libido up to a merry heat. She tapped his cheek.

"Be brave, lover boy. And don't trust him." Without so much as a glance in Raven's direction she managed to pinpoint the guy.

"He kept me out of trouble."

"That's the only reason he's still breathing.

"Come now. Talon will know we've passed this way." She took his hand and squeezed it tight. "Why don't we walk together a little way?"

13. THE CATACOMBS

Deal cautiously with the dead,
so that they might deal graciously with you
–Mrs Tunney's Words to the Wise.

ASHA HELD ON tight to Blaze's hand.

He didn't understand that she was clinging onto him to reassure herself he was still alive. Her heart was still doing a tambourine jig—*pitter-patter, pitter-patter*—like it had forgotten how to slow to a sensible rate. The relief when she'd come through the window and found him alive and standing had almost counterbalanced the horror at seeing the Wisht Hound's jaws around his arm.

Truly, she ought to celebrate his penchant for leather. If he'd been decked out in anything else... Well, it'd have been far messier, a bit like the gore in the streets. She was trying to blank out that particular horror. Not easy between her tearing rage at Talon for orchestrating it, despair over the lives lost, and her own guilt. Twenty-four hours ago she'd been part of the engine responsible for the slaughter.

How screwed up was her life, that it had taken a fledgling youkai prince to make her see the truth and step away from Talon's madness? She'd spent years slaughtering demons, but it had only taken a few hours of Blaze's company to strip away most of her prejudice.

No. No, that wasn't true. She still thought they were a serious threat to humankind, and when it came down to it, she didn't consider Blaze one of them. Not really. Blaze wasn't like any other demon she'd ever met. Admittedly, most of the ones she had met hadn't lived long enough to impress her with their personalities. In her mind, a good demon was one whose blood was scattered on the breeze.

"Hang on." Blaze came to an abrupt halt. "This is going to lead us straight into the Death Ward. Don't we have enough trouble on our tails without playing parley with the dead?"

"Vervain will deal. Don't fret."

"I'm not fretting."

"Relax, Blaze. We'll skirt the edges."

The dead were the least of their worries. Above ground her former associates were running wild, and the youkai were likely still out hunting their prince, too. She couldn't allow him to fall into either set of hands. Problem was she didn't really know what to do with him, either. Their trip to the Eyrie hadn't gained them anything solid enough to formulate a plan on. It had just bombarded her with images she couldn't interpret.

Oh, and gained them a hanger-on she didn't trust.

She shot a backward glance at Raven. The

arrival of the Wisht Hounds, hadn't changed a thing. He still stank of wrongness. She closed her eyes, inhaled deeply. It was hard to pick out individual scents when Blaze's was so distinctive and overpowering, but there was definitely a trace of something she didn't like.

Actually he smelled of Blaze, as if Blaze had rubbed his scent all over him.

"Nothing weird happened while you were running, did it?" she asked.

"Weirder than running through a slaughter ground and being chewed on?" He met her gaze a moment and then bowed his head. "Nah! Not sure I could deal with any other shit."

Asha sought Blaze's hand again and the reassurance of physical contact. She gave it a squeeze. "Let's get somewhere we can discuss our options."

O NCE BEYOND THE stone-lined cellars of the shops and into the catacombs proper, the light faded to pockets of phosphorescent algae, and they were forced to walk in single-file, clinging onto one another's hands, whilst hardly able to see the floor in front of them.

Thankfully, Vervain seemed to know the way, so Asha allowed him to take point and sandwiched herself between him and Blaze, leaving Raven to bring up the rear.

If she was lucky, Raven would get jumped and she'd have one less thing to be concerned about.

Blaze's hand felt curiously warm in hers, heating her even through her leather gloves in a way that such simple contact ought not to. Her pulse continued to thud. It took a few minutes to realise the sigil burned into her palm was tingling too.

She did her best to ignore it, but there was no denying the increasingly persistent erotic ache in her loins.

Asha steadied her breathing and concentrated on their surroundings. Now really wasn't the time to be indulging in lust.

Phantasms leered at her from the numerous dingy side-passages. Bent and rusted bars blocked several of the tunnels, and behind each a scene from her past played out in the dark, all of them sexual in nature: Blaze naked and vulnerable in the cage in the cathedral, Blaze fighting her questing hands on Palter Rogers' sofa in the Archive of the Blessed Brethren of the Deceased; her hands beneath his T-shirt, sliding over the smooth contours of his chest; her desire for him so crisp she could taste it as clearly as if it were blood upon her tongue.

Then one image overlaid all the others. Last night, she and Jaku had brought Blaze to the cathedral unconscious. Even comatose, he'd been impossibly lovely, his torso bare and so pale. He was hairless, his nipples two mulberry-coloured steeples either side of the demon mark that identified him as the future prince.

When they'd laid him before Talon's throne, Blaze had looked every inch the fallen angel. His black feathery wings closed like those of a butterfly. Fragile. Mesmerising.

But Talon hadn't looked on him with love, or reverence. Instead, his blue eyes had narrowed to fine slits and he'd scowled and then laughed because the wind had brought him a great bounty. He'd used Blaze's essences—blood, tears and semen to usurp his throne.

She'd seen that look and wanted to fall over Blaze and cover him, protect him, but Jaku had held her back, and some of the other hunters had borne Blaze away and placed him in the cage.

Her memory leapt forward a pace or two. Screaming... Tearing... Her body so consumed with need she'd convulsed with the pain of wanting, whilst high on whatever toxic mix of youkai madness bonding with Blaze had infected her with. It was far worse and far better than any Blood Rain hit she'd ever had. Sparks had ricocheted up and down her spine, through her belly and limbs. Her breasts had been heavy, nipples tight. She'd wanted more of him. More time, more of his body pressed close to her, their limbs entwined, his cock thrusting inside her.

The lights in the cathedral chapter house had been dimmed to a single blue orb that illuminated Talon from the top down. The beads and bones knotted in the ends of his long blond hair sparkled like the traces of magic on his skin. He'd raised a hand and beckoned her. And fool that she was, she'd gone to him.

She'd bowed down and worshiped him, accepted him as a substitute, allowed herself to be manipulated.

Too well trained, that was the problem.

Talon painted a line of Blood Rain down his torso and had her lick it off, as if she needed an additional kick when she was already so far over the edge.

It had made her crazy...crazy for sex of any kind, even the kind Talon enjoyed. That meant screwing with her mind as much as physically possessing her.

Where was the fun in consensual? Talon wasn't interested in safe words and getting cosy and contented. He believed in living on the edge. In taking things to extremes and damn the consequences. If she hated him because he'd repeatedly made her beg him to fuck her, then all the better. It would simply make their next time together even sweeter.

"Will this suit for a while?" The husky hum of Vervain's voice jolted her out of the memory. "I daren't take you any deeper, not with nightfall so close." He led them through a door hidden behind a carved depiction of Gregor the Apostle. Light flared when they entered the squat chamber beyond, the yellow glow from two wall mounted lamps almost too bright after the black of the tunnels. Asha blinked, and sniffed at the musty air. Someone had been here recently enough for it still to reek of their sweat.

It was a dismal little space, barren apart from a single pallet, barely long enough for a man to rest on, and two carved wooden benches, so hideous even Talon would have balked at owning them.

"What is this place?"

"A contemplation chamber."

"What are you supposedly to contemplate, how fucking awful the décor is?" Blaze pushed between her and Vervain and dropped onto the pallet, which gave an alarming creak.

"We mostly use these chambers to test the

resolve of those seeking entry into the order. There are four or five of them scattered among the catacombs, some of them with less endearing neighbours than this one."

Hostile corpses, just what they needed. She knew Vervain was itching to get away, but was still tempted to hold onto him for another hour just so she could pin Blaze in a seat and talk to him about what to do and what the hell their plans were.

"You should be okay, but if you do have any trouble, I recommend hitting them hard and fast. Now, if you'll excuse me." Vervain bowed his cowled head, and Asha nodded in return. She didn't want to lose the copse-man, but he was going with or without her permission, so she'd best just acknowledge that fact.

"Wait." Blaze sat up with his shoulders hunched and his arms wrapped around his knees.

"I have to leave." Vervain's expression said it all. His narrow nostrils flared, and his chin jutted in a determined fashion. "The youkai have never been my concern."

"Even after what Talon has done?"

An image of the butchered corpses strewn across Hangover Street flashed across Asha's vision. She quickly blinked it away.

"Your war is not mine." Vervain folded his arms inside his robe. "The dead are eternal, and the gates of the Death Ward will be busy tonight. The ghostly hunters will march. They'll march to collect their recruits."

The Ghost Wind would swell the numbers in its ranks, as if the City needed another growing terror. Every night the windborne horde swept through the streets, chilling, strangling every living thing in its wake. Long had it been the perfect way to murder. There was no death penalty anymore, just a night in the gibbets by the crossroads. Come morning nothing of value remained, just a ragged corpse.

"Hmm—right!" Blaze dropped his chin onto his knees. "And your eternal dead—what happens when you kill them a second time?"

Vervain's drawn face relaxed into a smile. "Good question. Alas, I haven't the time for a theological discussion right now. Maybe in the future, Blaze, when you have the leisure of the throne, and I less of a harvest to bring in."

"Let him go, Blaze." Asha ushered Vervain towards the door. There was no point in prolonging this any longer, even if she did prefer him to stick around.

"Yeah, but how are we supposed to find our way out of here?"

"We're not going anywhere until daybreak."

Blaze looked set to follow Vervain back out into the corridor, except Raven moved into the doorway the moment Vervain had passed and blocked his way.

"Vervain, how do we get out?" Blaze called over Raven's shoulder.

"Turn right and follow the passage north. It'll bring you out on upper Steepleside."

"Right back where we bloody started again." Blaze's fists clenched in frustration. Asha felt it, too. She just hoped she was better at concealing it.

"Uhhh." Blaze thumped the doorframe to the right of Raven's head, leaving him shaking his fist in pain and a noticeable indent in the wood way out of proportion with his build. While no featherweight, Blaze wasn't exactly built either, but, damn, maybe his youkai heritage was riding closer to the surface than either of them cared to admit. Maybe she ought to check the tattoo, make sure it hadn't been damaged in the fight with the hounds. Thing was, she didn't want him to get all twitchy and suspicious so asking him directly was out; plus she didn't want Raven in on the discussion.

After a moment's silence, in which they all seemed to be digesting Vervain's departure, Raven, who had continued to occupy the doorway, threw a satchel onto the pallet Blaze had reoccupied. It contained cheese and an assortment of choice delicacies he'd obviously pilfered on the way through the delicatessens. "Get something to eat and rest up. I'll take first watch."

The hell he would. Asha stepped forward to intercept him, planting one of her gloved fists in the centre of his bare chest. He stopped and looked down at her. She hadn't realized it earlier, but she had to significantly tilt her head to look him in the eye.

"I'll be on the other side of the door should you need me," he said. The last bit aimed at Blaze, rather than her.

Blaze rose and pushed a knob of cheese and half a salami into Raven's fist. "We'll take shifts. Come and sit down, Asha."

She didn't trust him, but maybe outside the door was the best place for Raven to be, at least out in the corridor he wasn't cramping the conversation she and Blaze needed to have. Come to think of it, she could do with getting him back in here to investigate that ward mark he claimed he had. Huh—as if she actually believed that.

The thing was, when she sat down beside Blaze and his lovely scent wafted over her, talking was no longer foremost in her mind.

14. BLOOD RUSH

DOLL HAD HIS number and no mistaking. She'd had her beady bloody eyes on him from the moment they'd met.

Raven hunkered down in an indent to the left of the door that he suspected from the green tint to the stone might once have been a water channel. Damned Talon, they were all as batty as a church steeple, and Asha was no exception. At least it made sense of their totally non-secret HQ. Every bleeder in the City knew they were based in the Cathedral, which meant he hadn't needed to use any of the extremely pleasurable, if technically unethical, methods usually adopted by his people when they needed information from humans to discover that information. Although, perhaps there'd been a little of that, just to make absolutely sure the details weren't duff.

He did wonder if it was actually safe to leave Blaze alone in there with her.

Shit only knows how she'd managed to persuade him to let her ink him. Then again, Blaze clearly wasn't himself. Something big had obviously gone down while he'd been incarcerated in the blasted Hall of Ancients. Something so big that he suspected his prince had actually been reborn. The alternative would necessitate Blaze being so exceptionally devious it was actually impossible to see through the layers of haze he'd constructed to get to the truth.

Raven took a bite of salami and chewed slowly, welcoming his taste buds back to life after an exceptionally long vacation. Sadly the sausage didn't remotely compare to the sizzle he'd got off Blaze's blood earlier.

Blaze had always satisfied like nothing else. The times when they'd properly been allowed to... He blanked the thought from his mind. Not going there—so not going there.

Raven's one regret over his punishment was that he'd been parted from Blaze. He had no idea how long had passed. Presumably, considerably more years than the ten he'd been meant to serve. He supposed everything had changed in the youkai realm, where passions and alliances transformed with the phases of the moon. Still, that seemed the place to head. It would certainly be safer than here, where they were sitting ducks for Talon and his pretty marionettes. Not that Raven went for the funereal, dead concubine look. He preferred his women a little sumptuous, and a hell of a lot more vocal. Asha could out-silence a silencer. Why'd she need words when she could just stare you to death?

Doll was probably staring holes in the stonework right now, trying to keep an eye on him. If it weren't for Blaze's obvious attachment to her, he'd probably have taken her out by now...

The lady was trouble and no mistaking. Big trouble. He just prayed Blaze had a handle on her.

"THE EYRIE DIDN'T exactly work out the way I'd anticipated." Asha cautiously began.

"Don't sweat it, I'm used to disappointments." Blaze brushed his knuckles along her thigh. It was clearly intended as a comradely pat rather than an affectionate one, but that didn't stop the prickle of excitement from spreading under her skin. She watched him tip out the contents of the satchel and run through the assortment of goods, sectioning them into meat, veg, dairy, and pastry.

"Blaze, what happened with you and Mr Knuckleduster?" She nodded her head towards the closed door, just to make sure he got that she was alluding to Raven. "Up in the Eyrie, and after I told you to flee the plaza? You were supposed to stick with Vervain, you know."

Blaze picked up a pimento filled olive, sniffed it, and then discarded it in favour of a marinated chicken thigh. "Not sure Vervain was so keen on sticking with me. He's been hanging pretty tight with you." He offered her a bite of chicken, which she declined, but leaned over to wipe a smudge of spices from his mouth.

"Not interested," she said. Fact was, it didn't matter how much danger they were in or how much she told herself this was the ultimate in a list of bad ideas, she still craved Blaze. Vervain was never going to turn her head. Talon hadn't managed it. So why would anyone else stand a look in?

Her itch for Blaze hadn't abated since their first kiss, which he'd later admitted he'd only initiated in order to prevent her discovering the demon mark on his chest. Now she only had to be hip distance from him for her libido to crank into overdrive.

Youkai poison, she knew that's what it was down to. Hell, she'd had enough years of experience to know what a Blood Rain hit could do, and she'd got the poison straight from the source, so to speak. Overindulging the human desire for sex was how the youkai infiltrated human society. Taking a demon lover to bed guaranteed kicks you weren't going to get elsewhere. Not that anyone did willingly take a demon to bed—except her—because the trouble was they didn't know when to stop. She'd seen more than one half-eaten victim who'd fallen foul of the youkai's lust for blood and their appetite for fresh meat.

Blaze had bitten her. Only the once, but—the terror, and the tight desperation in her sex flooded back to her. Even then, she'd still wanted him. What's more, she'd take that risk again. Over and Over. Until she couldn't take it anymore.

"A SHA—ARE YOU okay?"

Blaze saw her blink, but he wasn't sure she'd actually heard him. She'd been staring into space for several minutes, refusing the food he offered.

She needed to eat. Raven was shit hot in the field but Blaze still considered Asha their main defence. She was quicker than the demon and she didn't waste time playing with the enemy. That and well—he trusted her. Whereas him and Raven...let's see... there were still too many unknowns he needed to unravel first.

"Asha." He stroked a stray hair from across her brow and cupped his palm around her cold cheek. The green of her eyes shone, but he wasn't sure she was actually seeing him either.

"Oh, fuck!" He'd seen her like this before, when she'd been high on the poison that ran through his veins. Human—demon, it was a toxic mix. He ought to get away from her. Let her sleep it off.

Blaze almost withdrew his hand, but at the last moment his determination faltered. He'd tried to leave her once before and hadn't been able to. It was ludicrous to suppose he could do so now, especially when she leaned into him, until her black painted lips touched the skin of his neck.

Her heat. Her scent. He didn't want to fight her off.

She didn't stay focused on his neck long. Her attention turned to his face and she rained kisses down upon his mouth.

Hell! "Asha... I shouldn't be doing this with

you." He ought to stop it, push her away or something. She wasn't in control of herself.

Except he couldn't. Just wasn't able. Instead, his hands clawed in her skirts, and dragged her closer, and closer, until she straddled his lap.

He wanted her... a taste of her flesh, a drop of her blood upon his tongue. The sudden urge to bite almost overwhelmed him. Blaze held himself impossibly still, quietly breathing in her scent, all too aware of the pressure building behind the fly of his leathers.

Asha shimmied closer, lifted herself and ground against the hummock made by his erection.

Cool it! said his brain.

Shame the rest of him wasn't listening.

Her hands slid beneath his T-shirt, over the site of the skewed tattoo and the demon mark on his chest, almost as if she were checking they were still there. When she reached the latter, a buzz started in his head, and the sigil flared white-hot again.

It hurt. It always hurt. Such pain. Exquisite agony. Every time he thought it would completely overwhelm him, his body responded with an accompanying ripple of pleasure.

Blaze traced the line of her jugular with his lips. It was so tempting just to latch on and take a little bite. Instead, he dragged his focus away from her neck to feast on the swell of her breasts instead.

Asha had beautiful breasts, each a perfect handful. He had to unwrap them from the layers of satin and lace she dressed in, but that made it all the more fun. There was something especially appealing about the way the two pert orbs jiggled as he released the top four or five hooks of her bodice. His cock bucked against his fly, reminding him it too was eager for release.

Blaze pressed his nose into the channel he'd created between her breasts and melted into the warmth. It still wasn't enough. He had to have at least a part of her in his mouth. He scooped one breast free of the binding and claimed her nipple. The little expulsion of breath he heard her make made him suck a fraction harder.

Asha sagged against the wall to the side of the pallet. One hand clenched within his hair.

"The world's falling apart and we're fucking." Her voice was distant, as if she weren't entirely present.

"Yeah. Yeah we are."

He was surprised she'd even spoken. He didn't want to talk. Blaze kissed her again to silence the flow of words, assuming there were any more to come. Dammit, she tasted good, a sublime blend of dark chocolate and exotic spices. He didn't want to let go of her, but he seriously needed to release his zip.

Asha beat him to it, her gloved hands wrapped around his shaft. That was a kink too far. He wanted the sensation of skin on skin. "Take the gloves off."

"I'm not sure that's wise."

"None of this is wise. Take them off."

She did, tugging the fingertips with her teeth, and casting the gloves onto the floor.

Blaze shrugged off his jacket and pushed his leathers down around his knees. He got off the low bed and knelt between her thighs. Asha watched him, her attention absolutely focused on his face. Blaze slid his hands up the length of her boots; not stopping when he reached the top, he progressed up her stocking to the bare skin of her thigh.

Her mons was covered by a single wisp of fabric. He hooked two fingers around it and snapped the lace. She whimpered as he shoved two fingers into her heat. She was wet, sticky and sweet with need.

She spread her legs wide as he dipped his head and licked her. Bending to do so was the last rational thought he had, and definitely the last human one. Not that he was particularly focussed on his emotional radar.

Blaze worked his tongue and sucked her clit until her every breath was a purr. Then, and only then did he kiss his way up her body to claim her lips.

Asha wound her legs around his waist and dragged him down on top of her, so all his weight pressed against her. She wouldn't let him rise, seemingly determined to lock them together so tightly it was no longer clear where they each began or ended. He could feel her every breath as if it were his own. Each jerk she made, even the slight tensing of her muscles in anticipation of his entry.

He locked them together, taking, giving, making them one.

Making them one...

He realised something had changed when the mark on his chest blazed into life. It had been pulsing for a while, niggling at his senses, but the moment they'd joined something changed. The pain mounted tenfold, but so too did the pleasure. He couldn't stand it, but nor could he bear to end it by pulling away.

"Asha!" They were both bathed in pale blue light. He was riding so close to the edge now, fate sweeping him along, although he sensed there was still time to pull back, to make a different turn.

He didn't want to pull back.

She was calling his name, screaming with pleasure as her orgasm caused her to convulse around his cock.

Shaking with need, Blaze fought against the blindness that was his future.

The horizon was dark...

Why was it always dark? What had happened to the sun?

The noise of hammering, beating drums pounded in his ears. Wails rose in the background and the scent of charred wood filled his nostrils. Blaze's focus remained straight ahead, although he sensed other bodies behind him. Back up?

Asha wasn't among them. He wasn't sure how he knew, but he was certain of it. There was a void where her emotional signature should have been.

They were on a bridge, a damn long bridge that seemed to stretch between the stars. The Old City lay before him, burning like the heart of an enormous ruby.

He stared at it, fascinated by the colours and the heat, but he didn't run. He kept his pace steady, planted one foot before the other...thud, thud, thud, regular as a heartbeat, the sound right inside his head...thud, thud. Slowing now. Slowing and becoming fainter.

"Blaze, let go. You've taken what you needed. Now release her."

"Huh?" He shook himself, and the dingy contemplation cell snapped into focus again. It had been his grandmother's voice calling him. He almost expected to see her, looking at him and shaking her head in disappointment at his ways. His grandmother had never had time for the Talon. Why would she care what he did with Asha? However, there wasn't as much as a breath of Grandma's presence in the dismal cell.

The pain hit him hard. His fingers clawed as the skin across his shoulder blades split. Black wings fanned from his back. Blaze crumpled, off balance. He didn't think he'd ever get used to their weight, and the way the air tickled his feathers. He landed on his knees, eye level with Asha draped across the bed.

She was covered in blood. Hers? His? He really wasn't sure. Just that it was everywhere.

"Asha, I'm... Fuck, I'm so sorry." He looked down at his spent cock in disgust and then wrenched his leathers up. She was so still. Absolutely still. Had he bitten her? Hell, he wasn't sure what he'd done.

When the door creaked behind him, Blaze swung around in alarm. Raven crossed the threshold, his expression stern and his thickly muscled arms folded across his chest. He glanced at Asha on the bed, before sliding his gaze over to Blaze.

"I can explain. I mean, she's okay, isn't she?"

Raven dropped onto one knee beside the bed and sought the pulse point in Asha's throat. "She'll be fine. You've just exhausted her. Humans—they don't have the stamina. The blood's mostly yours," he added after a brief pause. "You're transitioning. How long have you been living as one of them?"

"As a human? I've told you already, I'm not a fucking demon. I've been with them, as you put it, all my life."

"You were reborn," Raven said. "That's what happens at the end of one cycle and the beginning of the next. Each time the Blood Moon rises. You change. That time must be close."

"I know the Blood Moon is fucking close, that's what all this crap is about. It could be up there shining away with its red filter now for all we know." The reminder of blood stopped him short, and he dropped to Asha's side again. Her pulse was strong, if a little unsteady. He had bitten her, hard and deep by the look of it, enough to leave her with a big fat bruise, and possibly a permanent scar. Blaze ran his tongue over his teeth. Every one of them was elongated and sharp.

"I—I fed on her."

"She taste good? Then what's the problem?" Raven shrugged and then strolled away. "Clean up, chill out some, and try and lose the wings. I'll take your watch."

"How? How do I lose the wings?"

"You'll figure it out—" the burr of laughter tainted Raven's voice, "—my liege."

15. METAMORPHOSIS

"How you doing out here? Any sign of trouble?"

Raven glanced up at his liege lord, whose wings were now retracted and his clothing back in place, although a trace of blood still remained upon his lips. "It's all quiet. I reckon the dead are busy about town, doing their shopping or whatever it is they do of a night." He didn't pay that much attention to human ghosts.

"Kill people," Blaze replied. He straightened his jacket. "Devour them whole."

"Urgh, that's just not right. Liver is nasty." A broad grin stretched across Raven's face.

Blaze rolled his eyes, and dropped onto his bum beside him in the narrow alcove.

Raven immediately stood.

"What?"

"You're my prince."

"Oh, for fuck's sake, sit down. You weren't such a stickler for etiquette earlier." Blaze waved him back to his stone perch, which he resumed reluctantly. Now he was upright, that seemed preferable to an ice cold butt; the damn stone was sub-zero, a fact Blaze was apparently learning, as he wriggled, obviously trying to find a comfy spot. There weren't any, he'd already spent an hour searching. Raven hunched down again beside his lord, and his shoulder rubbed against the sleeve of Blaze's jacket.

"So, I'm your prince. How come you're only acknowledging that fact now?"

Raven shrugged. It had taken a while, between the Talon, the slaughter, and the dog for the situation he'd woken to, to properly sink in. His initial pleasure at seeing Blaze had been eroded when he'd realised his old friend wasn't entirely with it. Somehow he had to jog Blaze's memory, get him thinking and acting like himself. Hell knows, rebirth happened to all of them at some point and Blaze was among the oldest of them, but timing-wise, this seriously sucked. And whose bright idea had it been to locate him in the City among the humans, instead of keeping him safe within the palace?

"Raven?"

"Sorry, yeah. We've been friends for aeons, it didn't sink in how much time had passed, or that you really had no memory of me. Seems weird. Guess I'm not sure what we are now."

"So you've fallen back on the formal."

"Yeah." That and he'd bothered to use his sight and seen the truth of things. It would be difficult to maintain the distance though, if Blaze insisted on them hunkering down together like this for quiet chats, with hardly a breadth of a gnat's arse between them.

"Aren't you cold?"

"Nah, I'm good. Always run a bit hot."

"So, we're friends?" Blaze asked, although it sounded more of a statement than a question.

Raven tentatively nodded.

"How come I punished you? You didn't think I'd forget that bit, did you?"

Nah, he hadn't forgotten, but he was starting to think there'd been a whole lot more to it than he'd originally thought.

"So?"

Raven shrugged off the prompt. "I screwed up. I'm not even sure why it was such an issue. You're a right secretive bastard, with all due respect, your highness. You keep your own council. It's the one of the few things you and Talon have in common."

"Don't compare him and me."

"Okay, no offence." Raven raised his hands to fend off the snarl. Fact was, he was wondering how much of the current situation was tied up with his punishment. What he'd done had been pretty minor, and Blaze's reaction completely out of proportion, but who was going to challenge his decision.

You wanted me out of the way. You knew what was coming.

Damn, he was sure of it. Bastard had probably planned his own absence from court, too. Though hell knows what the reason for that was.

"So obviously the wings are only part of it, are you going to fill me in on the rest?"

Despite the reassurance he'd just given,

Raven shivered. "I can only answer for what you were. I don't know what you are now. You've been reborn. Things change."

"That's a cop-out if ever I heard one."

He'd seen lovers of centuries turn on one another and fight to the death, and those with little more clout than a foot soldier reborn as gods. Maybe that's why Blaze had arranged his absence from court. Time to adjust to the change. That didn't explain the memory loss, or why he'd been masquerading as a human for so long. Assuming anything Blaze said could be relied upon. If he'd deliberately blocked his memory, what's to say he hadn't implanted a few details to fill in the gaps and ease the transition?

Raven rubbed his bicep again, where the raven's head curved across the muscle. "Wasn't much you couldn't do if you set your mind to it, but as I said, things change. What have you noticed?"

Blaze gave him a guarded look from under his eyelashes. "Just some killer headaches. Oh, and I'm ravenous again."

Headaches were probably to do with a memory bind, or something similar. Appetite was normal. Sex and flesh—the humans weren't wrong on that score. Being ravenous was tantamount to being alive for an adult demon. Guess that answered the unspoken question about whether Blaze had wolfed all the food or not.

"Mind if I ask you something?" He noticed Blaze eyeing him curiously again.

"Go ahead."

"How'd you hook up with her? I mean, she's an

odd choice for a pal, and weirder one still as a lover. The youkai and Talon... Well, it's been going on forever. It's not going to end until one side or the other is wiped out."

Blaze sucked his tongue a moment. "Just happened. We only met last night. I was attacked and she was there."

Speaking of attacks, he snuck a glance at Blaze's arm. There was no need to ask how the dog bites were healing up. He could tell they were fine from the way Blaze was using his arm. One more thing his liege would be hiding from Talon's bitch, assuming she recovered from the banquet he'd made of her.

"Attacked by who?"

Blaze pushed his hands into the spikes of his white-blond hair. "Demon by the name of Venom. Do you know him?"

All thought of food instantly vanished. Raven heaved as if he'd been punched in the guts, but managed to save face by turning his shock into a long and elaborate cough. "Aye," he said. "Did she kill him?" It took every ounce of strength he possessed to keep his voice steady, and even then he winced in anticipation of the answer.

Blaze shook his head. "No, he carved open my back and left me for dead. That's not to say he didn't come back later for another go. Nearly skewered me with a glaive that time. Third time he took a different tack, wanted to get all chatty, only Talon dropped in too."

"Talon..." Damn, he couldn't even say it. He knew this wasn't going to be a K.O. encounter. *Hell's bollocks.* He coughed. "Reduced to dust?" That bastard was going to pay, and pay dearly.

"Gone?" he repeated, just to make sure he had it straight.

"Yeah. Out by the old railway sidings."

"Shit!" And he wasn't even in a position to go and scoop up his brother's remains, and save him from becoming part of some damn alchemist's cocktail, or cut with rust and sold by the ounce to fools with neither sense nor decorum. However, preserving the prince's life was more important. If he'd been concentrating on that in the past instead of screwing with him, maybe his brother would still be breathing, and he and Blaze would be sitting in the Hall of State planning an attack, instead of running scared in an oversized rat run.

Besides, it sounded as if he'd be too late to save Venom's remains. Damn bleeders had a nerve decrying the evils of his race. At least the youkai didn't snort human remains for a fleeting high.

Blaze rubbed his jaw as if searching for stubble. "Were you sent to find me?"

"Blaze, I've been locked in the bloody Hall of Ancients for forever. It's pure chance you stumbled upon me."

At least he hoped it was. If Blaze had deliberately planted him there as part of some scheme, he and his liege would be having serious words later, rank notwithstanding. "You're sure you don't remember a thing?"

"We've been here already. Blaze Makaresh, age twenty-three, orphan—"

"—cute arse, nice hair," Raven finished for him. "Yeah, I remember. Nothing about our world?"

"Our world?"

"Okay, that's a big fat no." Raven stared at the smear of blood upon Blaze's lips, tempted to lean in and remove it, and maybe jumpstart Blaze's memory while at it. In the end, he held back. Best not risk destroying the bridge they were building before the foundations were even set. He didn't want to freak the devilish bastard out. He was on edge enough, and even if this was all a ruse, it was probably best to play along and see it through rather than risk provoking a rage.

"So, have you and her got any plans on where we go from here?"

Blaze's attention drifted towards the opposite wall of the corridor, where clumps of luminescent algae had grown inside grooves in the stone. Each glowing mass resembled an eyeball. "We haven't discussed it yet."

"Then, if I can make a suggestion? We should cross the bridge and head for the palace. It'll be safer while you're figuring out what's what, and considering how imminent the moonrise is, you ought to be rallying the troops."

"Bridge?" Blaze cocked his head. "Palace?"

Even in the dim light, his eyes glowed like burnished copper, so beautiful and expressive. Amber and bronze flames flickered in their depths, mesmerising him with their innocence and intensity. Was it any wonder Blaze had always been a popular leader?

This was getting downright difficult. Blaze's memory was just one big blank, like he'd had his entire past sucked out of him with a vacuum cleaner. He had to try and do something about that. Maybe taking his liege home would spark something.

"We need to cross the Division Bridge, Blaze. I really think I should take you home."

Blaze gave him a look of bemused disdain. "To someplace I can't remember? Wonder what the welcoming committee will be like. Surely if I've been absent someone will have stepped in to fill the vacuum."

Valid point. Not easily argued against, except that niggling doubt about Blaze's supposed twenty-three year history of living in the Birdcage. All his instincts screamed at him that it was a fabrication. The guy had probably lived there six months tops. Not that he saw any point in expressing the opinion. Blaze wasn't going to take it on board, truth or not. He was still carrying too much of a torch for his fictitious grandma.

You had to be brave or else suicidal to suggest love like that was a lie.

Raven held onto the thought. Now wasn't the time to suggest it, and if he could get Blaze's memory back, there wouldn't be any need for him to act as the assassin of lost love.

"That's a hell of a lot of ruminating you're doing over such a simple question."

"Yeah, sorry. They'd stand down as soon as you reappeared, assuming anyone has stepped into the power vacuum." Well, with a bit of persuasion they would.

"You realise that doesn't paint me in a very good light. What am I, some sort of tyrant? I'd have to be pretty vicious if you're saying no one is even going to consider usurping my throne in my absence."

"It's not like that, Blaze." A smile broke across

Raven's face. "You're getting it all back to front. Your people love you—mostly—you're good to them. That's why there are no malcontents plotting coups behind your back."

He could see Blaze remained unconvinced from his sceptical expression, even before he added the weight of a dismissive "hmm" into the equation. So, fine, Blaze wasn't a saint, but none of them would have wanted that anyway, and the truth was there'd been no real challenge to his authority. Youkai society didn't run on the same system of political manoeuvring and backstabbing humans used. Everything was far more hierarchical and precise. Blaze was their prince by circumstance of his birth, and by merit, and that was the way things would remain, unless he genuinely ceased to exist, which was not at all the same as being reborn.

"Will you come to the bridge?"

"I should see what Asha thinks."

"What she thinks? Blaze, you're a demon! She's doing her damnedest to pretend you're something else. Do you honestly think she's going to agree to this?"

A flash of blue showed through the copper of his irises. "That's as maybe, but she needs to know what our options are, and this is only one option. She may have an alternate suggestion."

"Hide in these dismal little rat holes until the sun fails to rise and the Blood Moon is upon us. Have you never considered that she may actually still be loyal to Talon, and she's here to make sure you're unprepared and incapacitated?"

"She's not."

"Blaze, she trapped you in a human skin. If we

hadn't stumbled upon one another, you'd have torn yourself apart."

"That was an accident, a misunderstanding. She was trying to protect me."

"From what—being yourself?" Raven briefly bowed his head. He rose to his feet and stretched out his cramped legs. "Don't mistake good sex for sound politics. She's Talon, and she's swallowed more than one of our kind before now."

He turned his back, leaving his liege to ponder the broader implications of his parting shot. It was hard to respect anyone who snorted, tasted, and generally imbibed the remains of your kin in order to get high.

They'd head for the bridge, with or without Asha's approval. If he had to sacrifice her in order to keep Blaze safe, he would.

ASHA WAS FLOATING. She wasn't sure who or where she was anymore, maybe heaven, if such a thing existed. Her neck ached—hell knows why—and fountains of colour sprayed across her field of vision. Numbers, names, places, burst onto this vista as splashes of vibrant orange, magenta, and blood red.

Maybe she'd been cracked across the head from behind. She wouldn't have put it past Raven to do that. Except there was no painful lump.

The weight of Blaze's body pressed against her side. His scent filled her lungs, sustained her as though it were the air she needed. She felt weak...so very weak. It was an effort to move. She struggled to raise a hand to her brow. Fat teardrops of sweat peppered her forehead. Fever. She had a fever. That explained the weakness, and why her tongue seemed to fill her mouth.

"Water," she groaned.

The shape beside her didn't respond. Not even after she'd prodded it.

Asha slowly opened her eyes. The room seemed dark after the kaleidoscope of colours on the inside of her eyelids. A satchel lay beside her in place of Blaze and a black feather with a bright pink aura lay upon her chest. "Water," she croaked again, patting her hand across the covers to find the flask she normally carried. Her long skirts were tangled around her hips, and a long ladder ran down the length of her stocking and disappeared under the top of her boot.

At least her boots were still on. That was good. She'd never liked fighting barefoot. She was always too conscious of her footing and you never knew what you were going to wake to.

Finally, her pawing paid off. Having snagged the flask she took several long swigs. *Better. Definitely better.* Even if it did taste like a frog had come in it.

She attempted to slosh the taste away with a bit of saliva, then set to work fastening the hooks of her bodice. The creases in her skirts vanished the moment she let the heavy fabric fall around her legs. Thankfully, her weaponry—bar the sword and the knife she kept strapped to her right thigh—was where it belonged. The remaining items were soon relocated. That simply left her the problem of what had happened to Blaze.

Both the room and the corridor outside were

ominously quiet save for a steady drip of water. The ting as it hit the rock floor echoed unnaturally loud. Asha stared at it, surprised. Not only was it drum loud, each time the water hit the floor the room flickered out of focus.

More sorcery? "Blaze!"

Something weird was going on. Even weirder than normal, and she lived weird.

She swept into the passageway, still conscious of the lethargy remaining in her legs. A bit of exercise would work it off. Maybe this was still the after effects of the doggy poison.

"Blaze?"

"Here." His legs and then his shoulders appeared from an indent cut into the wall several feet from the doorway.

"What are you doing out here? You're not supposed to take a turn at watch. Where's Raven?"

"Right here, keeping my beady eyes on him, so you can stand down. It's all safe."

She turned on the spot to find the other man behind her. He'd commandeered a shirt from somewhere, white—well, maybe a long time ago—and baggy, with an open V at the neck, so the beak of his raven tattoo showed through the gap along with a fair expanse of musculature. Strange that he seemed to have grown more brawn since they pulled him out of those vines.

"Time to move on," he said. "We were just waiting for you to wake. Blaze thought we'd better consult you over where to go."

Blaze turned his palms upwards and shrugged. "I just wondered if you'd learned anything up in the Eyrie that might guide us. It was the point of us going there."

Yeah, up until he'd turned it into a save and rescue mission.

She frowned realising she could see coloured auras around both of their forms. Raven passed her and went to stand by Blaze. It was weird, like someone had crayoned around their outlines, only the colours flickered and changed.

"You needn't scowl. I just wondered," Blaze remarked.

"Oh. No, nothing. Nothing useful, anyway."

"Okay, so what if we headed up to Steepleside and took a look around?"

"Hmm."

Raven leaned against the wall nonchalant as you please, right by Blaze. The closeness between the two men made her hackles rise.

"If it's all clear we could make a dash for the bridge."

Yeah, sounded reasonable enough, except for the black flash across his aura, like a stripe of deceit.

"Why the bridge?"

He shrugged.

"Do you know anyone in the Heights?"

"Nope." He shook his head for emphasis. Hair that was still friggin' perfect. Damn, how did he do that? He had to have a pot of hair wax and a mirror stowed in one of his pockets, alongside the gun he'd miraculously produced. They still need to talk about that little marvel.

"It's out of Talon's way."

Reasonable assumption, if not entirely accurate. Talon's influence extended into several seemingly unlikely places, including the glittering vistas of the Heights and the show homes of the rich and glamorous.

The thing was, trekking down to the bridge made her nervous. The Division Bridge was exposed. Just a flood-lit road and a river, a long drop off the sides, and not much else. The houses ended a long way from the river bank. It was a no man's land, and like the crossroads, a frequent battleground. She and Jaku had clashed with far too many miscreants on that bridge for her to ever consider it a choice destination. Plus, once they reached the Heights, they were going to stand out in a big way, unless Blaze had some cocktail outfits stashed in his pockets, too.

"I'm not sure heading there on foot would be entirely safe." The best way to cross the bridge was generally on the back of motorbike on account of it being quicker.

"But it's possible? I mean there are archives in the Heights we could go into. There might be more information there. It's where I originally stole that copy of the Apostle's Dialogue from."

"You mean the one that landed you in all this trouble. I don't know, Blaze."

Why, since he was presenting such a clear option in favour of going, was there such a murky tinge to the swirling mass of colours around his body? Did that signify anything more than an emotional investment in the answer? Why could she even see these fields? Something to do with the damned sigil burned into her palm? She tugged at the cuff of her glove, making sure the mark was covered up.

"All right. We'll head for the Heights." Having a

destination would at least keep them focused, and the Heights was as good a place as any right now. "Immediately?" she asked Raven. "Or do you need to rest?"

"Nah." He clapped Blaze hard enough across the shoulder to dislocate bones, yet strangely Blaze didn't budge an inch. "I'm good."

That, she seriously doubted.

16. ONE STEP AHEAD

JAKU TOOK A deep breath before he strode forward towards the dais where Talon sat crossed legged upon his throne in the nave of the former cathedral. Hard to believe what he'd done. Harder still to look at the guy he'd done it with. Just because he'd dreamed of it, fetishized it to the umpteenth degree didn't mean he was comfortable with the reality. Skin on skin contact—a shiver rolled through his body at the memory. He'd have preferred to stay dressed. Instead, he'd been exposed and forced to acknowledge his own form, and the scent and sensation of sweat upon his skin as they moved against one another. The thought of being placed in that position again both thrilled and revolted him. So did the scenes upon the streets.

The Old City stank of freshly butchered meat, and its old fashioned, open stone gutters ran with blood. To these arterial canals the city's vermin had flocked to feed. Rats, carrion birds, even a few of the winged youkai they'd been sent out to slaughter.

He was no longer waiting for the Blood Moon. Hell, in one form at least, it had already arrived. It simply had an alchemist master in place of a demon prince.

"What news of your partner and her demon whelp lover, Jaku?"

The way Talon wound his name around his tongue and turned it into a sensory embrace overrode any implied negativity over his past association with Asha. Fact was, he should have followed his instincts and decapitated Blaze when he'd had the chance. Not that he truly regretted the situation. One action led to another, one little change had a waterfall effect. If he'd killed Blaze, chances were Asha would still be in Talon's bed instead of him. And no matter how much being exposed made his skin crawl, he wouldn't change that.

"I assume from your silence there's no word of them."

"Hangover Street, not far from Maggot's, we found the hounds you sent out."

"Hangover Street. So, they've gone into the catacombs."

Jaku inclined his head.

"Why didn't you follow?" Talon asked.

Aside from the obvious fact that he valued his life.

"They're accompanied." He knew Asha's handiwork, just as he recognised Blaze wasn't responsible for the other deaths, not unless he'd metamorphosed into somebody with a fighting brain and some hard-earned experience in the last twenty-four hours. That and there were other issues.

A complicated knot of emotions tightened inside his belly. Jaku released his hair from its leather restraint, letting the inky strands fall across his face like a mourning veil. Honestly, he didn't want Asha found. For years they'd made a good team, took care of one another, stood back to back in battle, and bound one another's wounds. He might not agree with the decision she'd made to flee Talon's side and take up with the alleged prince of the fiends they'd spent years hunting, but he didn't want her dead, or worse still, back here in Talon's possession. He couldn't blame her for wanting her freedom. Blaze was entirely incidental to her desire to flee. It was hardly her fault she brought out the worst in Talon, and hence inspired endless fascination.

"You're right to fear for them." Talon's smile shredded his nerves like the screech of metal against metal. The elegant bastard shook his mane of blond ringlets, so that they bounced around his shoulder catching the light of the foot high candles that lit the nave, but his eyes remained cold and fathomless.

Damn him! Talon was probing inside his head again. His thoughts pushing and poking at the blockades Jaku had erected as he'd patrolled the streets.

They weren't quite strong enough.

Talon didn't even aim for the cracks. He effortlessly punched holes through the walls, which meant the bastard knew exactly what he'd been trying to hide, and why he hadn't pursued the rag-tag and bob-tail group beyond Maggot's.

"They've been inside the Eyrie!" The arrogant smile dropped from Talon's face. His spine straightened and his fingers laced before his face. "Blaze Makaresh has no power worth speaking of, and Asha even less. The prophecy makes clear..." He shook his head. "Not until the Blood Moon rises could he even attempt to break the warding on those doors."

Jaku backed away, as Talon, now on his feet, stormed down the dais steps. "He has some ability, Talon. Don't forget he shattered the wards on the cage you held him in and the glass in the rose window." His gaze briefly strayed to the window above the cathedral door through which Blaze and Asha had made their escape starting this whole sorry affair. Still without its glass, the wind whistled between the jagged shards that remained in the frame.

"Child's play. They had help. Who did they have help from? Who does she know that speaks the old tongue with any fluency?"

Despite Jaku's back-stepping, Talon stood directly before him. He reached out and grabbed the lace frill around Jaku's neck. "Who, Jaku? You know, don't you? Who do you honour besides me?"

"No one...no one, I swear it." He did his best to drop onto one knee, but Talon held him upright.

"I can see the deceit in your eyes." He stood for a moment punching bricks out of Jaku's feeble mental barricade. Jaku had no honour. That was why he'd ended up a starveling and frail. From birth he'd been destined to follow his father's path, become ordained as one of the Death Wardens—the jet eyed copse men. From the moment of his birth he'd been afraid.

He and his sister's roles should have been reversed. She loved the strictures of their society. He flouted every rule; more often than not accidentally, although his rejection from the order had arisen through wilful rebellion.

He'd entered the tomb. He'd made a mockery of their rituals and dishonoured the dead, and not just any dead. He'd slighted the thirteen princes of the old kingdom, made a den from their bones and used the rags they were dressed in as a canopy. He'd played chuck stones with their knuckle bones, and a whole host of other violations. He remembered the extensive list as it was read out to him. With one childish act he'd destroyed his family. The punishment—eternal servitude. He owed Vervain his life; he'd turned a blind eye when Jaku had chosen to run rather than face the penalty of his crime.

He didn't realise he was crying until Talon caught his tears upon his fingertips. He followed the caress with a kiss.

"Vervain." Talon plucked the name of the man who had both saved and damned him from his lips. "Jaku, you told me you were an orphan when I took you in."

"I am. My family are gone." They walked the city at night as part of the Ghost Wind, waiting for him to atone for the shame he'd brought upon them. His transgression demanded a tithe, and since he had flown like a coward, scared, and unwilling to face death, his family had settled the debt. All of them, every last one.

"You introduced them?" Talon asked.

"She was with me when I spoke to Vervain once or twice while following leads. They are not close friends. If he acted, it's because it fitted his purposes to do so."

Talon leaned close again, so that the vivid blue of his eyes filled the whole of Jaku's vision. "I have a rival?"

"No." Jaku shook off his hold. "No. Absolutely not. Vervain's interests don't run to the living."

"Then why help? Is he allied with the youkai?"

"Hardly. There are no funeral rites to administer."

"Hmm... well, no matter." Talon turned his back and strode back towards his throne. "They'll emerge topside soon enough. I'd like you to take some backup and go down to the bridge."

The bridge? "What for?"

"To stop Blaze from crossing it."

Okay, obvious answer; except he couldn't see why Blaze would want to head into the Heights. There wasn't a single soul up there that wouldn't sell him out for cash or a whole host of other dirty goods.

"Why are you still here?"

"Doesn't make sense."

Talon resumed his throne, and scooped a pocket-sized folio with an ox-brown cover from the floor. "You should read more Jaku then you wouldn't ask such pointless questions. It's part of the prophecy." Talon turned the book around to show the pages, not that Jaku could make sense of the ancient text. "The bridge between worlds. Now go bring me the whelp's head. Asha, I want alive."

17. MAUSOLEUM

**
"Do not mess with the Ghost Wind.
Do not disrespect the Ghost Wind.
Do not enter the Death Ward unattended
unless you're looking for a permanent residency."
–The Book of Death, Lesson 1.
**

ASHA BROUGHT UP the rear of their little triad as they traipsed the long dark corridors, while keeping her hand clasped tightly around the hilt of her sword. It paid to be prepared. Who knew what they'd find. Might be bad, might be good, might be darned invincible. In which case she'd be running and dragging Blaze by the collar if necessary.

The exercise was doing her good, but blots of colour still decorated the two men.

Raven led with Blaze before her carrying the torch. Shadows bled across the leather of his jacket, although she could still see his butt well enough to make her smile.

She hung back, trying to keep a little distance between them, because every time Blaze passed within six inches of her, her heart rate doubled and heat suffused her loins. More disturbing still, Raven had begun to have the same affect.

Asha lifted her focus to the design painted on the shoulder of Blaze's leather jacket, a crow against a red sun. He was certainly fond of crows. His first jacket had been fringed with black crow feathers.

Over his shoulder, she watched Raven rebind his dark hair with a leather thong. That man still troubled her, perhaps because deep down she knew all her suspicions were justified. Certainly, he had his explanations for everything, like this supposed ward that helped him heal. The ward mark didn't explain why he smelled of Eau de Youkai though.

She kept telling herself the scent was entirely down to Blaze—he smelled weirdly good, in a toxic, otherworldly, don't-mess-unless-you-want-your-life-wrecked kind of way—but, hell if that was much of a comforting thought either. She'd had him tattooed in order to stop the transition. Yet, his scent was definitely getting stronger.

Blaze noticed her scrutiny and gave her a weirdly troubled smile. Perhaps, he didn't realize it, but he rubbed his abdomen as he did, which served to further focus her attention.

"I thought Vervain said this was a straight route out."

"Aye, but he didn't say he'd been down here recently." Raven finished binding his hair, and poked at a bit of dislodged flooring with his toe. The farther they'd walked, the more dusty and unloved the corridors had become. Most of the original brickwork flooring was misaligned, causing chunks of rock to stick out of the ground at angles. The phosphorescent algae that made navigating the pathways earlier almost bearable had disappeared half a mile back, leaving them with a single torch to light the way. There was nothing living in this part of the catacombs, not even an earthworm or a bug, and it had been growing colder for the last half mile, too. The lintel above Raven's head lay shrouded beneath a layer of frost. Further ice crystals decorated the walls in geometric patterns.

"We must be directly below the main cemetery." Blaze dragged a finger across the pattern on the wall, leaving behind a greyish trail. "What time of day is it? Does anybody know? How long have we been down here?"

Asha shook her head. It had been early evening when Vervain had led them below ground, but still daylight. She had no idea how long she'd slept after she and Blaze had… whatever it was they'd done. They didn't want to be heading out onto Upper Steepleside with the Ghost Wind still howling.

"Why don't you two stay here a bit? I don't like the feel of this." Raven actually looked perturbed. He found a bone and bound a rag around it before lighting it on the torch Blaze held. "I'm going to check up ahead. The roof is sloping downwards and what we've just passed through isn't exactly structurally sound. Temperature is still dropping, too. I think things might have altered since Vervain last came this way."

Blaze wouldn't meet her eyes once Raven had gone. He started poking around, looking into the cubby-holes that lined the passageway at fairly regular intervals. Most of them were blanketed in ice, with no more than a glimpse of skeletal remains behind, and the odd link of iron chain.

"How are you feeling?"

He glanced over his shoulder at her. "I'm fine."

"Sure about that? What about the arm?"

He winced as he looked down at the sleeve of his leather jacket and the row of tears where the Wisht Hound's teeth had penetrated the hide.

"Blaze." She grabbed hold of him, squeezing tight around his supposedly injured arm. He yelped in protest, but not in agony. "Show me that tattoo," she growled into his face. "Tell me what happened in the Eyrie when I left you alone with Raven. Or was it on the streets afterwards?"

"Nothing happened."

"Liar!" Asha wrenched up his top. At first she thought everything was fine. It was only when she properly focused that she realised the pattern had been skewed. What looked like a set of razor sharp claws had torn through the design in four parallel lines, and then instead of healing straight the wound had knit off kilter.

"Was it him?" she demanded. As if she needed the confirmation. She knew Raven was responsible. She'd been right not to trust him. "He's one of them? He's Youkai, and you deliberately hid it from me. I can't believe you let him stay with us."

"Asha, I'm one of them."

"He's made you change. You were stable...human."

"Am I? Your friends were performing this chant. I couldn't think...couldn't react. My head was going to explode." Blaze shouted, which somehow quietened her reaction. For a moment she could almost feel the intense pressure Blaze claimed he'd experienced, and that had blotted out his vision. "He saved me."

Asha froze. She could hear his heartbeat. She was holding his arm, but there was still a foot between their bodies. Besides, this wasn't just the feel of his pulse. She was hearing the steady, somewhat excited beat of his heart.

"Asha, I can't hide anymore. I'm grateful for everything you've done, but I have to accept what I am. Who I am. You can see that, right?"

She just stared at the inked design where it swirled around his belly button. He'd been so pretty, so innocent when she'd met him, now he had battle scars, and there were lines around his eyes that hadn't been there before.

The centre of her left palm tingled.

Blaze bent and wedged the torch into a rut in the floor, and then he pushed his hand into the strands of her hair that hung loose from the elaborate knot upon her head. "Don't hate me for it."

Hate him. She could never hate him. She looked up at him, into eyes that were no longer blue, but copper.

"Blaze, have you thought this through? If you stand against Talon... You've seen the prophecy... You'll bring burning rain down upon the city. The humans you've lived alongside will be herded like cattle and fed upon."

"It won't be like that."

"You'll lose your humanity."

"Will I? Have you considered that Talon has already disposed of his? That the city is in mourning tonight because of him. I didn't kill those people on Hangover Street, Asha. I won't be blamed for their deaths. That was Talon's doing not mine. The only person with a death agenda is him."

"What has Raven said to you? Has he told you the Youkai plans?"

"There are no plans, beyond crossing the Division Bridge."

"Aren't there? What's over there? Have you asked him that? What's so important about the Heights?"

Blaze sucked in an extra deep breath. His hand moved from her hair to her cheek, where his thumb stroked along her cheekbone. He still had kohl around his eyes, which emphasized the metallic sheen of his coppery irises. Did he even realise his eyes had changed colour?

"What is it?" she asked.

"We're not going to the Heights. That's not where the bridge leads."

"It doesn't?" She sceptically raised one brow. She'd crossed it often enough and it hadn't ever led anywhere else. "Last time I looked it went straight to swish apartment central."

"It's the walkway between worlds. I have to cross over, Asha. It's not safe for me here. Talon will scour the city until we're found. It's better that I'm out of his reach."

"Damn!" She couldn't argue with that. It would absolutely be better if Blaze were out of Talon's reach, but she also needed him to stay human.

"Blaze, don't do this. Don't give up."

"I'm not. This makes sense, Asha. I can't do anything dead."

Her breath stalled in her lungs. Talon would kill him.

"We can go together. You can keep me straight."

"Yeah." She wanted to believe that. She really did.

No way was she crossing that bridge. After years of slaughtering youkai, her name and face were well known to them. Even returning their prince to them wouldn't outweigh her past crimes. Better she took her chances with an enemy she knew intimately. There were still places within the city she could hide. She still had a few friends of sorts who might help her out.

Blaze's caress reached her lips, and the simple touch seemed to ignite her senses in the same way his nearness had done back in the contemplation chamber. She gasped and he leant forward to kiss her.

This was going to be goodbye.

S HE DIDN'T WANT him to kiss her like this. Not with tears running down her face making the taste of him salty, but she couldn't let go. Blaze held her tight against his body. Ferocious heat rose off his skin. Her hands found their way inside his jacket and under his T-shirt to curl against the smooth muscles of his back.

Fever hot—damn youkai with their fiery blood.

"No." The cry escaped despite her best effort. She'd only just found him. It couldn't be time to end it already. And yet, they'd been running from the moment they'd met. And all appearances and wishes aside, he was a demon.

Oh, shit! That's why she felt so woozy. She should have recognised the symptoms. She was high on him, reacting like every other blasted human idiot she'd had to save over the years. This is what sex with the youkai did. It got you hooked.

If Blaze noticed her tears, he didn't show it. He kept on teasing her lips and tugging her closer, making her want more than just the kiss. She dug her fingers into his flanks, and felt Blaze smile. Then he lifted her and pressed her back against the wall. His kiss dropped to her neck, and was followed immediately by a sharp stab of pain.

Asha yelped as blood trickled down the side of her throat and into the cleft between her breasts. Blaze licked at the trail, before latching back onto the wound he'd made and seeking more. She could feel his tongue working, rasping against the raw nerve-endings. It was horrid and perversely exciting. The speed of his pulse had doubled. She shut her eyes and it was as if he'd crawled inside her skin. They were breathing as one, her pulse a thud that echoed his.

He was consuming her. If he didn't stop, she'd dissolve into nothingness.

Asha struggled in his arms. She wanted him. But not like this. Not so out of control that their appetites were getting the better of them. Oh, but his touch... it did things to her insides that weren't right or proper, and made her want to give in, to relax into the moment and throw aside all her reservations, maybe even ballista the iron fortress around her soul.

She lifted a leg and wrapped her thigh around his hip. Blaze clutched at her, supporting her, pulling her closer, while trying to release his fly one handed. Her hands were there too, releasing him, guiding him. She needed this. Hell yes. It was goodbye, and she wanted to remember exactly how good it had been.

His cock butted between her thighs and the sigil on his chest flared white-hot. Asha eased away from its fire, but a similar light streamed from her palm, visible around the wrist of her glove.

She didn't know who to blame for the connection, because she couldn't absolutely swear when the sigil had appeared upon her hand. Maybe it had been in the archive at the same time Blaze had discovered the demon mark on his chest, maybe it had come later after they'd had sex. Either way, it had bound them in such a way that made his touch impossible to resist.

His lips traced hers, softly, slowly this time. Was he trying to hold himself in check?

That surprised her, given how forceful he'd been a moment ago.

"Asha." He slid into her, going deep with a single thrust.

Too much! It was too much. She whimpered even as the muscles of her sex pulled him deeper. All the colour trickled from her field of vision. She was seeing him in black and white. All except for his eyes, they blazed with the fire of a thousand suns. He was inside her, and she could hear his caresses, his thrust like a strand of music; violins, the bows drawn lovingly across the strings. All her senses were crossed. She laughed and the sound filled her mouth with the taste of violets.

Blaze jammed a hand between their bodies and worked her nub. Damn demon, got it just right, too.

He was perfect. Fuck it. He was perfect, and she didn't want to lose him. Talon had abused her for years, made sex into nothing more than game of one-upmanship and deceit. It wasn't fair she had to let Blaze go so soon.

It wasn't fair... But life had never been that.

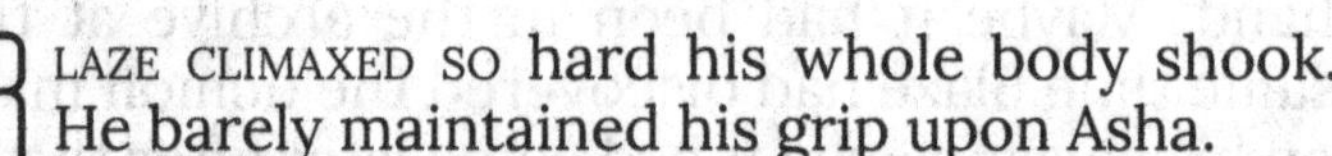

BLAZE CLIMAXED SO hard his whole body shook. He barely maintained his grip upon Asha.

The frost on the wall had melted away from the heat and friction of their bodies. It was a second of two after he came that the pain hit. He crumpled, fire flowing through his veins again, as though his blood had transformed into molten lava. At least there were no wings this time. Had to be grateful for that small mercy. The wings would make him vulnerable, more vulnerable than he already was, with his trousers down and his nerve endings alight. He'd never had the opportunity to acquaint himself with the aerodynamics of the two great feathery appendages, which meant his balance was off whenever he was on the ground, and then there was the small problem of sensitivity. The lightest breath blowing over his inky quills was enough to have him horny as a rutting stag. Someone actually ruffling his feathers... that was...well, it was the sort of ecstasy that fried your senses and turned you into an angel with a one-track mind.

"Oh, fuck!" Asha was staring over his shoulder. "Put me down."

He didn't question her. He did as instructed, and not a moment too soon.

"Duck right." A sword swept over his head, shaving off a few strands of blond hair.

Fuck was damn right. Four of the buggers were heading for them, glinting metal raised in bony fists. Four of them! Not good odds, not good odds at all since he was next to useless in a fight and Asha seemed a tad off kilter.

She's just come, you moron, of course she's off kilter.

What happened when you killed something that was already dead?

Vervain had never given him an answer.

"Take my knife, or use the gun you're carrying."

The foetid stink of the rotten flesh that still clung to the bleached bones of the skeletons assailed his nostrils and made his stomach heave. Blaze pulled the gun from his pocket. The cold weight of the metal in his hand didn't lend him any confidence.

"Shoot, Blaze. Don't stand about. Aim for the head."

She rolled left, came to a stand before two of the four, and thrust the knife that had appeared in her off hand through the ribs of the first. Blaze aimed for the one that came tearing towards him. It seemed wrong that an animated corpse could move so fast, when it lacked muscles and tendons and all the other things that normally drove propulsion.

Aim for the head. Aim for the head. Good suggestion, it was the largest solid target, if you took into consideration that a bullet would probably go between its ribs. Blaze pulled the trigger. The expulsive jerk ricocheted right up his arm. Damn walking corpse just grinned at him, the bullet clamped between its yellowed teeth.

Fucking crap!

Rather than firing again, he reversed the gun and hit the bastard thing in the face with the butt. Hell, if it worked on elephant-sized dogs, why not on a skeleton?

A demented grin stretched across his face making his cheeks ache as the corpse back-stepped under the force of the blow, spitting out its two front teeth along with the bullet. He hit it again, taking out a sliver of what little already remained of its nose. The third hit snapped its collarbone, causing its head to flop sideways.

Too bad he wasn't quite so nimble on his feet as Asha. The second skeleton dove under the arm of the first and made a grab for his throat. Blaze lurched left, stubbing his toes on the uneven floor. He regained his balance, but not before a white skeletal claw grasped his forearm.

Raven emerged from the dark of the tunnel. He threw the torch, which caught on the ragged remains of the cloak the skeleton wore. The whole thing ignited in seconds. Raven kicked it through a sheet of ice covering one of the cubby-holes. "Aim for the neck and then crush the skull."

He leapt towards Blaze.

Having obviously taken Raven's advice, Asha

sent a bony head rolling, which Raven cracked open with his foot.

The whole macabre dance flashed across Blaze's field of vision as if in slow motion. The bite of cold fingers upon his arm clicked something together in his brain. He concentrated, pulling together the pulses of energy that flared behind his eyeballs and at the back of his skull. Then when the pressure seemed too intense to bear, he released it as one massive breath. Bone shards rained against the wall and floor like hail. Both Asha and Raven raised their arms against the splinters, managing to avoid the worst, although they were both nicked and grazed.

Three down, one to go. They closed up, forming an unholy trinity around the remaining corpse.

"Blaze?" Asha asked.

He shook his head.

She and Raven nodded at one another. Their swords slid one over the other, neatly severing its head from its spine. Blaze chased the skull. A large drop of water splashed his face as he raised his foot to stamp down. Blaze looked up, instead. All across the ceiling, the layer of ice had cracked. The glitter of frost was gone too from the walls. More water splashed his upturned face. "The ceiling... It's coming down."

The ice split right over Asha and Raven's heads.

ASHA LOOKED UP in response to Blaze's cry. Time seemed to still then speed up inexorably as the ceiling split. She raised her arms, only for a shadow to lurch towards her and knock her off her feet. Rubble thudded around her, leaving her at the centre of a dust cloud. A warm body crouched in a protective arch over her body; legs spread either side of her thighs. Raven's chest pressed tight to the hooks of her corset.

Asha coughed and blinked, the spikes of a colossal headache stabbed through her brain and into her sinuses. She needed a drink and a cool dark room to lie down in. Instead, she had several stones of hot male above her, and what felt like the head cold from hell coming on. The shape hunched over her, raised his head. Hair as dark as her own, brushed her cheek. "Raven," she choked.

He pushed up onto his knees, causing a spray of glassy ice shards to slide from his back and splinter in the dust. He'd saved her. He knew who she was, what she was, and yet he'd saved her.

"Why?" They both knew the depths of that question.

"I swore to protect him. You're important to him, and we need you if we're going to get as far as the bridge."

She met the demon's mismatched eyes, noticed the amethyst flare in the one on the right.

"What do you see with that lamp-like eye of yours?"

He grinned, showing her enough fang to make it clear he was letting his true form penetrate his human guise. "The truth."

"And what truth do you see when you look at me?"

That bastard smile of his elongated another inch. "You love him. Fuck knows why, but you do."

The statement left her momentarily mute. Truth... that was the thing about the truth, people rarely spoke it. Did she love Blaze? How did you know when it was love, rather than caring for someone or just lust or poisoning? Vervain had accused her of the same thing. Jaku had always told her she was a cold hearted bitch, meaning it in the nicest possible way, of course.

She and Blaze had been through a lot together in the short time since they'd met. She could tick the boxes for both care and lust. It was just that last box causing such a headache. Maybe this wasn't the time to think it through right now. After all, why screw herself up any more than she already was, when they had other things to dwell on and they were heading towards a goodbye anyway?

"He feels the same way, except he doesn't know about the so long yet."

"I can't cross that bridge and you know it."

"I know it, and he doesn't have to. If he thinks you're staying behind he won't go, and he can't stay here Asha. Talon won't let him live if he catches him." Raven brushed the remaining dust and ice from his shoulders and then extended a hand towards her.

Asha warily eyed his palm. "I don't like this. What he's becoming? What you are making him into?"

"This is a guise, Asha. I'm not making him into anything new. He's simply becoming what he always was, and what he's destined to be again."

She took a deep breath and then accepted his

hand. His temperature ran as hot as her own. Together they rose.

"You're not like the others of your kind. I know them." She'd killed a fair few. "They're different. Different taste and smell. You smell of—" she sniffed.

Raven cut her off, "You haven't tasted me. Unless you sneaked a bite while I was out cold."

Tension immediately returned to her shoulders. She glowered at him and tugged her hand free of his hot grasp.

Raven gave an awkward snort, not quite bemused, more borderline nervous. He might, in not so many words, be declaring this a truce between them, but that didn't mean they were comfortable with one another.

"However, you're right. Most likely those you've encountered were foot soldiers. I'm an aristocrat. Different caste." He tilted his head, as if listening. "Is that scraping?" Between where they and Blaze had stood, there now lay a wall of rubble. "Blaze."

"He's fine," she said. "He's just trying to find a way through to make sure we're okay."

Raven didn't ask how she knew. He simply stared at her, with his left eye closed. Maybe she ought to be worried by that, except there were already too many things to worry about to make room for another. She didn't know how she knew, but she did know Blaze was safe. His heartbeat continued to drum strongly in her ear.

Raven began to dig from their side, and soon a thin thread of light pierced the gloom. It was only then that she realised how clearly she'd been seeing him in the dark.

"What's your night vision like?" she asked Raven.

"Fab."

And apparently contagious. Leastways, Blaze's was.

"You're not like any nobleman I've ever encountered," she muttered, leaning over Raven's crouched form to watch him widen the gap in the rubble.

"No?"

"No. They're universally a bunch of wet pansies, who wouldn't dream of getting their hands dirty. That and they're round, balding, and nine times out of ten, high as kites. Your kind seem to have a thing for them."

"Easy prey." He shrugged and laughed. "Over here, Blaze. We're okay. I gotcha." He clasped Blaze's hand where it poked through the narrow crawlspace they'd opened.

The light momentarily petered out as Blaze scrambled through. He seemed to have avoided the impact entirely, although the spikes of his hair were filled with dust.

"So what's your title then, noble boy?" Asha asked, as they watched Blaze dust himself off.

Raven pressed his tongue to his upper lip. "Head of the Prince's Elite Guard. That's the only title you need to know, Ms Concubine." He flashed her a smile. Too much smile. And she didn't think he was applying her title with reference to her relationship with Blaze.

It took a moment for the rest of what he'd said to her to penetrate the fog of colours still clouding her sight. The Prince's Elite Guard. Her gaze streaked towards Blaze, who was holding back now that he'd made it through the gap, looking unsure whether or not to intrude. When she turned her head towards Raven again, he gave her a barely perceptible nod. "Yeah, him."

Asha took a deep breath. There was no arguing with a truth like that. Demon had no reason to lie, not over something as important as this. They needed their prince, couldn't rule without him. She retrieved her sword and sheathed it, having first wiped the blade across the front of her skirt. The brocade was taking on a rather odd pattern due to the stains, as though a child had butterfly printed with blood onto a black background.

"Okay, what did you find? Is there a way through onto Steepleside?"

"Yeah. We're not far from the exit," Raven replied. He wrapped a shard of ice in a scrap of tattered fabric and pressed it to her brow. "Here, you're running a little hot."

Surprised, Asha took it. The cold sent a tiny shiver of relief down her neck and arms, and the swirls of colours momentarily blinked out.

"You're hurt!" Blaze rushed over and wrapped his arms around her, squeezing tight and nuzzling against the back of her neck.

"I'm fine, Blaze." She shot a warning glance at Raven, daring him to suggest otherwise.

Asha lowered the cloth from her brow and found it dotted with spots of blood. "Just a few scratches. Hey, you remembered what to do. Nice work with the skeleton."

Blaze scowled, clearly having realised the nicks were from the shower of bone, not the ceiling collapsing. When he tried to examine the nicks more closely, she pushed him away, so he turned to Raven instead. In addition to scores of grazes, the demon had one particularly cruel gash above his right brow, the blood from which had matted in his eyebrow.

"Okay?" Blaze asked.

Damn demon inclined his head a fraction, but his gaze stayed locked onto his liege's face.

"Good."

Blaze raised his hand towards Raven's lips, and her heart nearly damn stopped at the sight. Damned if Blaze wasn't aware of who he was too and enjoying it, but worse than the realisation that she could see him revelling in such power was the intimacy between the two men. Ties so strong she could see them as steel chains around them both. Jealousy crashed over her at the sight, so intense it had her literally seeing green—bright emerald green, a shade not unlike that of Talon's eyes.

"It's just a few scrapes," the demon protested.

"Two drops. Take it. We need to get moving, and we'll all fare better if we're not distracted by minor sores every few steps."

Raven bowed his head, then bit down on the tip of Blaze's index finger, and latched on, like a babe sucking at its mother's breast. Within seconds every scratch on Raven's skin had healed. Neat trick, shame demon's blood had never had the same effect on her.

Hot tears of anger and injustice threatened to fall. Asha blinked and her depth perception disappeared.

Unsteadily, she turned away and kept blinking

until her eyes watered and her vision calmed back down to a plague of colours.

A strong hand curled around her shoulder. "Are you all right?" Blaze urged her to turn so they were facing.

"Yes...yes, I'm fine." Like hell she was. Every time she looked at him her insides went into erotic meltdown, and right now she felt so fucked that if she lay down where she was, she wasn't sure she'd get up again for a week.

Blaze sensually sucked the wound on his fingertip made by Raven's eye-tooth. His irises were now a strange mix of copper and blue. "You don't seem... Well, you don't seen entirely yourself."

"It's been a shitty day."

"Yeah. Yeah," he sighed. "That's true."

18. THE DIVISION BRIDGE

"IT'S RAINING. I can't believe it's bloody raining." Blaze gave an exasperated shrug, which he tempered with what he hoped was an endearingly wry smile but was probably just goofy. He splashed into a puddle, kicking up a fountain of stagnant water that swilled over the hem of Asha's dress. "Sorry."

She didn't make a reply, barely seemed to notice the soiling.

"Reckon we should close that?" He nodded at the door that had just led them onto this forgotten back street of Upper Steepleside. They were in a small cul-de-sac, hemmed in by tenement blocks. Strings of washing wafted overhead, collecting the oily rain and blotting out most of the winter sky. The vista wasn't much improved at ground level. The ancient cobblestone road was missing many of its bricks, obviously pried up by the residents to patch holes in the boundary wall around the Death Ward. The only surprise was the door hadn't been boarded or bricked up on the outside, although, to be fair, it had taken their combined strengths to open it.

"I'm not feeling much love for the neighbourhood." He wrinkled his nose as the smell of damp and rotted fish wafted towards him from a mound of stacked crates.

Raven glanced up from the puddle into which he'd been staring. "Rain's the least of our worries. Take a look at the moon."

The silvery orb was reflected at his feet, and just a fraction off full. There was a definite pinkish tinge to its surface.

"I reckon we've three or four days at most."

"Two."

Blaze turned to look at Asha. That was the first word she'd spoken since she'd pointed out the day was shitty. Always made up to look perfect, the porcelain pallor of her skin had taken on a ghastly tinge, and the thick layers of kohl and mascara couldn't disguise the dark circles beneath her eyes.

"Two days and it'll be full, and demon rule will be upon us. Two days until you can claim your crown."

Curiously, rather than fill him with terror, Blaze found himself hard pressed to mask a smile. If everything came to pass as Kell's Prophecy suggested, then at least he'd get to kick Talon's scrawny arse, and if the alchemist needed one thing it was a damn good kicking. It might be nice to feel powerful rather than afraid, too.

"Anyone know the quickest way down to the bridge from here?"

Asha gently inclined her head. Most of the black paint had scrubbed off her lips, leaving behind a greyish residue that added to her wan appearance. "Up to the crossroads and then straight down the Demon's Causeway."

He'd always wondered why the road up to the Heights was called the Demon's Causeway on this side of the river. Sure there were some bastards living in the lap of luxury up in the Heights, but they were hardly flesh-eaters. Of course, learning the bridge spanned another boundary in addition to the river, one that predated the Heights by—he wasn't sure—centuries at least, meant it all made sense.

"The sooner we get you there, the sooner we can start planning," Raven said. The rain had already soaked through the grubby shirt he had on, rendering it transparent, so that the raven across his chest and bicep showed through.

Asha began walking, soon dissolving into the shadows that edged the base of each building. In her black finery she was nearly impossible to see. Blaze stalked after her, listening for the faint rustle of her skirts to follow her movements, and Raven fell in behind him, staying close.

They crept through several alleys to reach the main thoroughfare. The streets were deserted, doors and windows locked down tight, every crack and keyhole plugged fast to keep out the Ghost Wind. The people here didn't go out at night. They rose with the dawn and went to bed at dusk.

Sticking to the shadows and single file, they edged towards the crossroads, only speaking when it was absolutely necessary to do so. It was the wrong time of night to be abroad. The hollow moans of the dead singing their eternal lullaby drifted on the wind. Asha brought them to a stop in sight of the Lich Gate. Opposite the ornate wrought iron gate, a group of corpses huddled around one of the swinging gibbets. Within a crazed figure thrashed and sobbed in terror. "On my signal," Asha hissed to him and Raven. "We'll make a run for it while they're distracted."

Blaze's heart began a rapid patter, which sounded so loud in his ears he was sure the ghouls would hear it from across the street and leave the scrawny man in the cage in favour of some tastier meat. But their focus remained fastened upon the captive.

The poor soul, who had probably only stolen bread to fill his hungry belly or failed to pay taxes to some foul magnate in the Heights, began to scream: his howls of pain and terror were so loud, Blaze wished he could stopper his ears.

"Now." Asha waved them forward, and they slipped silently over the pitted tarmac. Only once they were in motion did it dawn on him why she'd chosen that moment. The man's screams stopped. Death had come and the hungry horde were feasting, tearing him apart.

"Run," Asha hissed, when they reached the end of the line of buildings and the canal drew level with the roadside. "Run, and don't look back."

It was two miles from the crossroads down to the river. Probably the quickest two mile dash he'd ever made. Every other trip he'd made to the Heights he'd done so on the back of a motorbike.

Blaze drew to a crouching halt between Asha

and Raven behind a line of marsh thistles. They were in the wetlands that bordered the river, surrounded by the chirp of nocturnal insects and the scent of marsh gas, when the lights on the bridge went out. Dark figures dotted its broad arch.

"Talon," he gasped, fighting to regain his breath after the sprint. How did they know this was where they'd be headed, or were they simply blocking every route out of the city? Blaze turned his head to face Raven. The tall demon crouched low among the grasses, seemingly oblivious to the water soaking his knees.

"Now what do we do? There are too many of them, we'll never get past."

"We don't have to get past."

"You said... Even if we just have to set foot on the bridge, it's too dangerous. They'll see us coming, and we all know they strike first and only bother with the interrogation if you're not courteous enough to die."

Raven's face lay in shadow, but his right eye shone in the dark, a bright flicker like a willow-the-wisp. "It's fine. We can do this providing the Ghost Wind doesn't prowl down this far."

"It won't," Asha remarked. "They don't come down to the marshes in case they get trapped here."

Baffled—in more ways than one—Blaze took another look at the bridge. It had to be fifteen feet above the river surface, and there was no other way of crossing save over its bowed back. At least twenty figures stood there, far more of Talon's dolls than he'd ever seen together. He wasn't even sure of their exact numbers; it had to be a sizable portion of Talon's force. Generally they worked in pairs, or trios. The only other time he'd seen such a big grouping was within the Cathedral while he'd been locked in that damn cage.

He wondered if Asha knew their exact number. It'd be useful to know how big a force he was likely to face if things ever got as far as a pitched battle.

"The other bridge." Asha spoke so quietly, he barely heard her. He followed the line of her gaze and saw she was looking downstream towards the Hardmouth Waterfall. "This bridge was built after the Heights sprung up. The original Division Bridge was a wooden structure."

Blaze squinted into the dark. Farther along the bank, low to the water, in the shadow of the concrete behemoth that was the current Division Bridge, a rotted jetty stuck out into the water. The mid-section appeared to have entirely collapsed and all that remained on the opposite bank were two stubby wooden posts. "That's it? What's left doesn't look solid enough to stand on."

Raven gave him a grim smile. "It's solid enough for our purposes."

Blaze blinked in surprise. He'd been half expecting Raven to contradict Asha's explanation and reveal another sturdier structure, or announce it could only be seen at certain times, or once you set foot upon it.

"No," he protested. "This is ridiculous. They're going to see us. We'll be sitting ducks. They're bound to have a few bow men."

To his knowledge, and the general incomprehension of the City's population, the

Talon had always eschewed the carrying of guns, preferring more traditional forms of arms.

"You and Raven go. I'll provide a distraction."

"Asha, no! It's too dangerous." He reached for her, grasped her shoulder, even as she moved to avoid the contact. Heat radiated from her, palpable through several layers of fabric. He pulled away again shocked. She wasn't just hot, she was feverish, despite the chill on the breeze that had numbed his fingertips and the end of his nose. "You're not well." He wasn't sure how she was even upright and moving.

"I'm fine, Blaze. If I'm hot it's because we've been running."

It wasn't just normal sweat cooling the skin of her forehead though. He remembered how she appeared to him—was it two or three days ago now?—when he'd woken to find her looking down upon him, everything about her flawless, her face scrubbed of emotions, mask-like. Now her skin was blotchy, and the make-up around her eyes smudged. She looked wild, on edge, ready to crack, yet there was also a wistful turn to her mouth as if she were lost in pleasant memories while a storm brewed around her.

Blaze opened his mouth to protest again. She didn't need a decoy mission, she needed bed rest. He wanted that too—hours spent beside her, his arms wrapped around her body so he could cradle her as she slept. However, Raven butted his head between them.

"It's our best option, Blaze. She knows what she's doing. She understands how they think and work, and I'll warrant she knows this area better than both of us put together."

"But they'll kill her if she's caught."

Asha shoved Raven out of the way. She inhaled sharply through her nose, held the breath a moment as an expression of grim determination etched its mark upon her face.

"Blaze, I'm a big girl. I've never liked this plan. I don't agree with where you're headed, but it's your choice. Personally, I'd rather you hung onto your humanity, and I don't think you'll do that in their realm." Her gaze flicked briefly to Raven. "But the fact remains that you'll be safer on the other side of the bridge, as far out of Talon's reach as you can get. I don't want to witness your execution, or worse, be forced to perform it. You need to go."

"I can't leave you."

"You're not leaving me. I can circle back to the bridge once it's safe. Talon has a third of his force on that bridge, he won't risk that many there come daylight, especially if he thinks we've already been driven back into the City."

"Asha, please."

"Blaze. Shhh." She pressed her index finger to his lips, silencing his protestations. "Jaku's on that bridge. I'll bet he's leading the group. Trust me, I'll be fine. He'll follow but he'll hang back and give me time to run."

"You don't know that."

"Yes, I do." The certainty in her voice surprised him. "Blaze, I've known him a long time. I know more about him than even Talon or Vervain, and there are plenty of reasons why he won't want me caught. If you were with me it'd be a different matter. You're a threat. Hell, I don't exactly trust you myself. You're youkai and not just a 'foot soldier'," she flicked a glance at Raven. "You're their Prince, the being supposed to bring slavery and destruction to my people. I've spent all of my adult life defending folks against your race. Don't make this more difficult. I'm struggling with the idea that this is the right thing to do already, believe me."

"I'm not going to destroy anything, Asha. I don't care what the prophecy says, that's not who I am."

"With all due respect, you don't know who you are. Everything could change once you cross that bridge. I saw what you were like before the tattoo tempered your appetites. You say you're not interested in domination or satisfying you demonic urges, but how many times have you bitten me now? You drank my blood. Don't think I don't remember it. I've seen the look in your eyes when we make love. It's hungry, Blaze, and it's not just sexual hunger. When that crazed youkai gleam enters your eyes, I'm never sure if you're out to fuck me or eat me."

"Listen to her." Raven elbowed his way into the conversation again. "We're wasting time. The longer we sit here debating the higher the probability we'll be seen. We need to move quickly and we need to move now."

"It's crazy."

"Let her do her stuff, Blaze. She understands the risk. She knows what she's doing." Raven's arm locked around his wrist and began tugging him away.

"Asha... Be careful." Blaze resisted the tug on his arm in order to pull her closer. His lips gently brushed her clammy skin. This was wrong. She was ill. He could see she was ill, but what other choice did he have?

"Blaze—take care. Stay low. Crawl down to the water's edge if you have to, then run, don't dawdle." She kissed him back, hard, bringing a throb of pain to his chest and the sting of tears to his eyes.

It wasn't cool to cry.

He took a deep breath and released her from the embrace. "Keep safe."

"Likewise. I love you, Blaze."

He didn't have time to reply before she was gone, a slim black silhouette moving fast against the deep magenta sky. When the first hollers of the watchmen reached them, Blaze took a step forward to follow her, only for Raven to hold him back.

"Trust me, she's better off alone than with you at her heels. She'll join us when she can."

He knew that, but it didn't do jack for the yanking sensation in his guts. It damn well felt as though someone had sewn a fishing hook in his innards and was now trying to reel him in. When Raven tugged him in the opposite direction it threw him off balance and he fell onto one knee in the shallow water. Blaze growled and formed a fist, but stopped short of swinging a punch. Brawling wasn't going to bring Asha back, or get them across the rickety jetty.

There were still figures on the main bridge when he and Raven reached the edge of the bulrushes. Luckily, their attention remained focused on their compatriots in pursuit of Asha. Was she right in thinking Jaku was leading the chase? From this distance the Talon all looked the same, like women, even though he knew they weren't. If it weren't for the gleam of sharp steel, with their fanciful outfits and white pan-stick complexions they'd look like they were on the way to some decadent gothic ball, not out to behead their enemies.

Close up, the rickety jetty resembled nothing more than four big sticks bound together with mud and fishing twine. Each of the supporting posts stood skewed at a different angle, while the boards they supported were green and black with slime. The whole structure extended no more than eight feet out over the water. "Damn bridge isn't going to support us. The only place we're going to end up is in the river."

"It'll hold. It might even surprise you." Raven smiled brightly, showing far too many teeth again. "And if it doesn't—you can swim, can't you?"

"If it doesn't, I'm going to damn well toast you in order to dry out."

"You remember how to do that and it'll be a big problem solved. We won't need to worry about the gothic dollies heading our way."

The Dolls weren't what was on Blaze's mind. Damned river was probably toxic, it smelled totally ripe, and a foamy residue clung to the reeds where the water lapped at the bank. If he went in, chances were he'd come out glowing and sporting extra toes.

Raven tapped his arm. "After three. Three...two... one. Now!"

Blaze lurched forward, partially off balance for the first few paces as they ran over the spongy grass and onto the shingle that surrounded the jetty.

If he had any sense, he'd been running in the opposite direction as fast and hard as his damn rubber legs would carry him. The shingle crunched and slid beneath his feet. White stones tumbled over one another and splashed into the water's edge. A shrill cry came from the direction of the main bridge, and then several lanterns bobbed over the side. "There! Down there."

Momentarily dazzled, Blaze barely resisted as Raven urged him onto the rotten boards. Five paces on and the wood splintered beneath his feet. He dived, and rolled along the remaining five feet of planks, where he rose shakily to his feet. Raven remained in the spot where the wood had given way and fallen into the river below, suspended on a structure—as far as he could tell—made entirely from fire and light.

Blaze turned a full circle. The flames now spanned the entire river, red, orange and lilac wreaths curled and interlocked with one another to form the walkway, while the sides of the bridge showed dancing and living figures, each one carved, as if in wood, but brought to life as fiery embers.

Beautiful. The whole damn bridge was beautiful, and strangely familiar, like he'd crossed it a hundred times before. The thing was, it lit up that entire section of the river. If they hadn't already been spotted, the lookouts sure as hell couldn't have failed to see them now.

Raven jogged over to where he stood. "You okay?"

"Fine." Blaze stared entranced by the flicker of

flames around him. He touched them, but they bore no heat. "The design, it's similar to the carvings inside the Eyrie."

"Same sculptor, for the most part. Your father."

His father! He'd never known his father. "How—how is that possible?"

"He lived plenty long enough before you crept into existence." Part of Raven's human guise slipped, so that when he smiled his teeth were sharp and pointed. His features appeared more elongated, too. Only his eyes remained unchanged; still mismatched and otherworldly. Raven squinted at him. "You do understand that your human grandmother wasn't real, Blaze? I don't pretend to know why you decided to reinvent yourself following your rebirth; I can only assume it was to protect yourself, but you have to disregard your human life. It's a lie. It's all been a lie. Hopefully, once we're across, your memory will return."

An arrow whistled past Blaze's cheek and hit the fiery handrail where it immediately dissolved into cinders. "What if it doesn't?"

"Worry about it later." Raven barrelled into his side, grabbing Blaze's arm in the process so he could sweep him further across the bridge. They were over the centre of the river when Blaze threw him off. He refused to accept the belittling of his grandmother. She had been real, no imaginary figment. She'd nursed him, looked after him. If he stopped and thought of her for a moment, he could almost catch the scent of the lavender soap she loved so much.

"Keep moving, Blaze. The bridge is vulnerable

while we're upon it. Get to the other side and there'll be no problem."

Whoa! "Hold up." If the Talon couldn't cross once they'd left the bridge, presumably because it would somehow cease to exist, then that meant Asha couldn't cross either. "Fuck!" He couldn't believe he'd fallen for it. Asha had figured it out. She'd known they wouldn't see each other again. It was why she'd kissed him as she'd done. She'd been saying goodbye.

He grabbed the front of Raven's stolen shirt. "She's not coming, is she? When did you tell her, or did she always know humans can't cross?"

"They can cross. In our company, while the bridge is open like this. It was her choice, Blaze. You have to understand that where we're going isn't the place for her. She's killed too many of us. Your people would demand recompense."

"She no longer supports Talon."

Raven pried loose Blaze's fingers from his lapels. "Two days of hot loving doesn't eradicate a decade of indoctrination."

"She hates Talon."

"Maybe, but look at the bigger picture. Do you really think Talon only learned about Kell's Prophecy two days ago? No. He's been planning this for years. Don't you find it a little odd that the Talon are without exception all male, except for Asha, the one person you just happen to meet and form a bond with?"

"She's no traitor."

"I never said she was."

"You deceived me, though."

"Blaze." Raven grasped the front of Blaze's leather jacket and violently shook him. "By all means curse me later. I've always been a treacherous bastard, but right now, it's time to run."

"Make that time to die, and you'll be a fraction closer to the truth." A husky voice intruded upon their moment.

Raven turned sharply, placing himself between Blaze and the four demon hunters who had formed up on the lip of the bridge with their weapons readied. Although their spokesman seemed eager to fight, the remaining three were eyeing the fiery walkway with deep suspicion.

Blaze pushed his hand into his pocket and grasped the cold metal body of the gun. If they dared come closer... A shiver trembled along his spine. He'd what? Two shots wasn't going to get him far, assuming he managed to hit, and every other piece of arsenal he had at his disposal was too bloody unpredictable. Last time he'd tried anything tricky he'd brought the ceiling down on top of Raven and Asha's heads. This time, hell knows, maybe he'd blow up the fricking bridge.

Raven reached backwards and yanked the sleeve of Blaze's jacket. "Go," he insisted without looking back.

"Not without you."

"Go, Blaze. I can handle this. There are only four of them."

Another arrow fizzled as it passed Blaze's ear. He didn't care how many hunters were after them, he wasn't legging it to the other end of this bridge without back up. Hell knows what he'd be heading into. That, and last count he only had a few folks he could genuinely call friends. He wasn't splitting on the only one remaining in anything resembling close proximity. "We retreat together."

"Right." Raven sounded wholly dubious. He took a step backwards as the enemy took a pace forwards. "You're a spectacular pain the arse, did I mention that?"

"Nice to see you've dropped the formal crap. What do you want me to do?"

"Besides run? Give me some space. I can't swing shit with you this close." Blaze shuffled back a few feet. He wasn't sure which scared him most, the four demon hunters out to separate his head from his shoulders or the fact he was standing directly over an ice cold river with only a flickering orange glow between him and a dunking.

The leader of the little group edged onto the bridge, leading with his sword, and backed up on either side by companions with pole-mounted billhooks. He'd seen depictions of the Talon in action with those things before, using the curved blades to snatch winged youkai from the sky, before stabbing them with the fluted metal base of the haft.

"Back up slowly," Raven hissed.

"Charge!" the lead demon hunter yelled.

"Shit!" Blaze wrestled the gun from his pocket, as the sound of metal grating against metal filled the air. He waited, steadying himself, seeking an opening, but with all the dancing about it was hard to get a bead.

With a mighty grunt and a screech, Raven threw his opponent backwards into his compatriots.

It was a split second decision. Blaze pulled the

trigger. The immediate kickback ran right up his arm, and went straight on up through his shoulder and kept going until his vision clouded over. He blinked, but the bridge faded out of view. The sky was no longer black bordering on magenta, but slate grey peppered with sulphurous yellow clouds. Thick fluffy flakes of ash filled the air, and sat in drifts across the rooftops and upon the cobbled streets.

Not now, he couldn't be here now. He had to stay in the present, help Raven.

He knew what was coming, the lightning that hit the cathedral rooftop and ran along the apex and into his flesh, the pain so exquisite and pure every nerve in his body sang. He convulsed. The wings inked onto his back broke free of his skin; muscles, tendons and bones rearranged themselves. Still the pain continued, so raw it stole his breath.

"Blaze!"

He toppled backwards only for someone to catch him.

Blaze stared up into the face of his saviour. Blobs of coloured light blotted out most of the male's features, although he got the distinct impression whoever his rescuer was, he was smiling.

"Need a little help?"

"Some. Upright would be good."

"Carry him," Raven yelled from the midst of battle. "Let's get the fuck off this bridge."

The stranger's smile morphed into a frown. "Well, isn't this a pleasant little reunion. Things have changed while you've been sunning yourself amongst the bleeders. You're not my boss anymore."

"Is..." Blaze mumbled. He had some vague notion of asking who the heck Raven actually was, but the rest of the sentence slipped by unspoken, as the man whose arms he lay in deposited him on his feet. Judging by his expression he'd taken Blaze's murmur as an affirmation of Raven's rank.

Blaze wobbled and grabbed the fiery handrail. The flames tickled as they curled around his palm. His vision had cleared a fraction, enough to realise the guy had wings, and some serious eyebrows.

"All right. I've got your back."

"Bugger my back, Sorrow. Get him off the damn bridge."

Blaze's stomach lurched halfway up his throat as the demon threw him over one shoulder so Blaze's head nestled in the space between the tops of the demon's tawny wings as he ran. The guy smelled of musk and engine oil, like he spent equal time tinkering with his motorbike and fucking. He struggled a little, and then relaxed. Where was he supposed to go, if not to his youkai "homeland"? Although, he'd have preferred a more dignified entrance.

He brushed his cheek against the smooth feathers of Sorrow's wings. The guy shook violently and dropped him. "You've got to be fucking kidding me! What are you on?"

Blaze looked up at the guy from his prone position on the floor. His tawny eyes were dilated into two perfect ovals, and a flush stretched across his cheekbones. He was breathing hard through his nose. Blaze matched his rhythm of inhaling and exhaling. He was seeing stars—actual, physical, twinkling around the other guy's head stars.

Raven caught up with them. His face splattered with blood and gore. "He doesn't remember. There's a whole heap of shit going on, and the Blood Moon's about to rise."

"Yeah, I got the last bit. Nice work by the way." Both demons glanced back along the bridge to where four bodies lay bleeding into the river. "Amnesia. How bad?"

Between them, they hauled Blaze onto his feet again. He smiled at them, only vaguely aware of their tight grips upon his arms. He was staring out over the city again from his perch on top of the cathedral roof.

There had to be some reason for the vision. If he could only figure out what it was.

"Pretty much every damned thing," Raven replied. "In short, we're screwed, unless the home visit rattles something loose."

ABOUT THE AUTHOR

MADELYNNE IS A New York Times & USA Today bestselling author. She wrote her first novel after discovering Black Lace Books in the 1990s. After escaping the Hotel California, she dived into storytelling full time. Her books are filled with bisexual bad boys who like to get down and dirty, and stories so angst-filled you know they're going to hurt.

She lives in the UK near the Welsh border, where you can find her surrounded by books, drinking rapidly cooling decaf coffee, and listening to loud music.

Come hang out with her via her newsletter, where she shares what she's reading, watching, listening to, and snippets about her current projects.

9 781917 284103